## MONTANA MAVERICKS

*Welcome to Big Sky Country! Where spirited men and women discover love on the range.*

### THE TRAIL TO TENACITY

Tenacity is the town that time forgot, home of down-to-earth cowboys who'd give you the (denim) shirt off their back. Through the toughest times, they've held their heads high, and they've never lost hope. Take a ride out this way and get to know the neighbors—you might even meet the maverick of your dreams!

Back in high school, Julian Sanchez watched from the sidelines as his more popular friend dated Ruby McKinley, the girl of Julian's dreams. Now they're all grown up, and Ruby is a divorced single mom with a toddler daughter and foster baby. As Julian spends time helping Ruby with her children, he realizes they might be the family he's always longed for. But Ruby is wary of another broken heart. Can Julian prove through words *and* deeds that their good thing is real— and built to last?

Dear Reader,

When the clock strikes twelve, Ruby McKinley has one resolution for the New Year: to be the best mom she can be to her four-year-old daughter. Shortly thereafter, an unexpected phone call leads to her amending that resolution to include a three-month-old baby boy.

Julian Sanchez can picture what he wants for his future, and Ruby and her kids are part of that picture. Of course, it's going to take some doing to convince the wary single mom to give him a chance—a task further complicated by the fact she used to be married to his best friend.

Love isn't always easy, and Ruby and Julian's fledgling relationship will face its share of challenges, including leaky dishwashers, spontaneous social worker visits, well-meaning but interfering family members and even an octogenarian uncle in search of his missing bride.

It's been a big year for the Montana Mavericks series as it marks thirty years of happily-ever-afters, and I'm thrilled to bring you Ruby and Julian's story as part of the celebration.

I hope you enjoy visiting Tenacity, Montana...and perhaps you'll see a long-awaited happy ending for Winona Cobbs and Stanley Sanchez, too!

xo *Brenda*

# THE MAVERICK'S RESOLUTION

## BRENDA HARLEN

Harlequin

MONTANA MAVERICKS

Special thanks and acknowledgment are given to Brenda Harlen for her contribution to the Montana Mavericks: The Trail to Tenacity miniseries.

**Harlequin®**
# MONTANA MAVERICKS

Recycling programs for this product may not exist in your area.

ISBN-13: 978-1-335-14317-4

The Maverick's Resolution

Copyright © 2024 by Harlequin Enterprises ULC

Harlequin Enterprises ULC
22 Adelaide St. West, 41st Floor
Toronto, Ontario M5H 4E3, Canada
www.Harlequin.com

**Printed in Lithuania**

MIX
Paper | Supporting responsible forestry
FSC® C021394

**Brenda Harlen** is a former attorney who once had the privilege of appearing before the Supreme Court of Canada. The practice of law taught her a lot about the world and reinforced her determination to become a writer—because in fiction, she could promise a happy ending! Now she is an award-winning, RITA® Award–nominated, nationally bestselling author of more than sixty titles for Harlequin. You can keep up-to-date with Brenda on Facebook and Twitter, or through her website, brendaharlen.com.

## Books by Brenda Harlen

### *Montana Mavericks: The Trail to Tenacity*

*The Maverick's Resolution*

### Harlequin Special Edition

### *Match Made in Haven*

*The Sheriff's Nine-Month Surprise*
*Her Seven-Day Fiancé*
*Six Weeks to Catch a Cowboy*
*Claiming the Cowboy's Heart*
*Double Duty for the Cowboy*
*One Night with the Cowboy*
*A Chance for the Rancher*
*The Marine's Road Home*
*Meet Me Under the Mistletoe*
*The Rancher's Promise*
*The Chef's Surprise Baby*
*Captivated by the Cowgirl*
*Countdown to Christmas*
*Her Not-So-Little Secret*
*The Rancher's Christmas Reunion*
*Snowed In with a Stranger*
*Her Favorite Mistake*

Visit the Author Profile page
at Harlequin.com for more titles.

For foster parents everywhere, with appreciation for everything you do and the boundless love you share.

And especially my sister and brother-in-law, aka "Mimi and Papa" to their Emy.

# Chapter One

Ruby McKinley didn't mind having to work New Year's Eve. Besides, it wasn't as if she had any better offers for the evening. Unlike her babysitter, who bailed at the eleventh hour when her sometimes-boyfriend invited her to go out, forcing Ruby to take her daughter to work with her. Thankfully, four-year-old Emery never complained about going to the inn with her mom, though that didn't make Ruby feel much better about it as she settled her little girl on the sofa in the manager's office with her iPad while she worked the front desk.

Though the hardscrabble town wasn't anyone's idea of a holiday hot spot, one of the event rooms at the inn had been booked for a party tonight. Ruby had seen the musical entertainment—the Row House Four, according to the placards posted on either side of the doors—come in earlier to set up for the party and had recognized one of them as Marisa Sanchez.

Marisa was a local piano teacher who'd become an internet superstar after a video of her multicultural, offbeat spin on the holidays had gone viral the previous Christmas. Ruby didn't know Marisa well, but the pianist's brother, Julian, was a good friend of Ruby's ex-husband. Her bandmates were apparently Marisa's roommates from her college days in Boston.

Ruby tapped her foot to the beat of the music emanating from behind closed doors and wondered what it would be like to have friends like Marisa had—friends who would travel halfway across the country to perform with her, just because she asked. Ruby was still in touch with some of her friends from high school and college in Wyoming, via the exchange of holiday cards and occasional text messages, but she honestly couldn't remember the last time that she'd met Lucy for lunch or had coffee with Shanice or even chatted on the phone with Caitlin. Of course, her friends were all married now and busy with their own families, and since Ruby's parents had moved to Florida, she had no reason to make the trip back to Wyoming.

Sure, she'd made new friends in Tenacity—including Megan Grant, the manager of the Tenacity Inn; Chrissy Hastings-Parker, who did catering for the hotel; and Lynda Slater, who'd selflessly offered both friendship and free legal advice when Ruby's marriage was falling apart. And while she enjoyed spending time with her friends when their schedules allowed, most of her hours outside of work were occupied by her daughter.

Suddenly, the music faded and the revelers in the party room began to count down to midnight. A quick peek into the office confirmed that Emery had fallen asleep watching her favorite Disney movie. Her wispy blond hair was splayed out on the throw pillow behind her head, and her hand was curled into a pudgy fist, her thumb resting against the lower lip of her Cupid's bow mouth.

Emery had never taken to a pacifier, but she did love to suck her thumb. And while Ruby liked to think she'd been making some progress in her efforts to break her daughter of the habit, there were occasional lapses—most often when the little girl wasn't in her bed at home, as was the case tonight.

The sound of noisemakers emanating from the party room confirmed that the new year had arrived, and Ruby lifted her can of 7UP in a silent toast to her daughter.

*Happy New Year, my baby—the very best part of my life. I've never been big on resolutions, but this year, I'm going to do better for both of us.*

The celebratory din began to fade, only to be immediately followed by another round of cheers. Before Ruby had a chance to speculate on the potential cause, Marisa Sanchez and Dawson John burst through the doors. The sound of cheers, whoops and a distinct *pop* of a champagne bottle could be heard in the event room.

Marisa waved her left hand in the air, the diamond on her third finger flashing in the overhead lights. "Dawson asked me to marry him—and I said *yes*." Then she turned to her fiancé and gave him a smacking kiss. "I feel like I'm the luckiest person in the world."

"Second luckiest," Dawson countered. "Because *I'm* the luckiest."

"Well, congratulations to you both," Ruby said sincerely.

And she was truly happy for the couple, who were obviously in love and excited about their future together. At the same time, she couldn't help but feel a little sad, because it didn't seem like so very long ago that she'd been the one showing off her engagement ring. That she'd been the one full of hopes and dreams for her life with the handsome and charming Owen McKinley—a life that had quickly fallen apart.

As she watched Marisa and Dawson, now surrounded by family and friends who'd spilled out of the party room into the lobby to offer their best wishes to the happy couple, Ruby found herself wondering if she'd ever experience love again…

Or maybe she should wonder if she'd ever know the joy of truly loving and being loved—because she'd recently found herself questioning if she'd really been in love with the man she'd married or just wanted to believe herself in love. Because at the time she'd met Owen, several of her friends back home in Wyoming had been planning weddings and preparing to have babies and Ruby, newly arrived in Tenacity, Montana, had been feeling alone and lonely.

And wasn't that a sad commentary on her marriage?

And perhaps proof that Owen had been right to blame her for its failure.

She pushed aside the unhappy thoughts, reminding herself

that her marriage was in the past and she was looking forward to the future, especially now, at the beginning of a brand new year.

And then every last thought slipped from her mind as her gaze landed on Julian Sanchez and registered the fact that Marisa's brother was making his way toward the front desk.

Julian had gone to high school with Owen, and he'd spent a fair amount of time hanging out with her husband when she and Owen were married, which was how she'd gotten to know the local ranch hand. He'd always been polite and respectful—albeit a little distant, until Emery's birth had breached that distance.

From the first minute, the little girl had him wrapped around her finger, and watching him respond to her daughter with such openness and warmth—a contrast to Owen's cautious disinterest—had filled Ruby's heart with joy. He'd been a doting and favorite "uncle" throughout the entire first year of her daughter's life, until Ruby learned about her husband's cheating and kicked him out of the house, resulting in Emery losing not only her father but also her honorary uncle.

Of course, Owen was entitled to visitation, and Ruby had been more than reasonable there. The fact that he rarely chose to spend time with his daughter was entirely on him. Thankfully Caroline and Mark McKinley—Emery's paternal grandparents—doted on their granddaughter and stepped in to fill at least some of the void resulting from her father's abandonment.

Ruby suspected that Julian's absence had left an even bigger void back then, but of course her daughter had been too young to have retained any memories of him.

But Ruby remembered him, and while he was obviously at the inn for the party, she had to wonder—why was he coming toward her?

And why was her heart suddenly beating a little too fast inside her chest?

It was possible that her physical reaction had something to do with the fact that Julian Sanchez was a seriously good-looking guy.

He was about six feet tall, she guessed—similar in height to her ex-husband. But that was where the similarities ended. Owen McKinley was smooth and polished and always immaculately dressed—his designer shirts neatly pressed (by the local dry cleaner, of course, because he couldn't trust his wife to do it right) and his ties perfectly knotted.

No one would describe Julian Sanchez as smooth and polished. He was usually unshaven, his hair seemingly always in need of a trim, his broad shoulders straining the seams of his Western-style shirts. But it was his eyes—dark and intense and full of wicked promise—that caused a woman's blood to heat inside her veins when they were focused on her. And his mouth—exquisitely shaped and quick to curve—that made a woman's knees quiver when he smiled at her.

Of course, she meant any *other* woman's blood and any *other* woman's knees, because his friendship with her ex-husband had made her immune to Julian Sanchez.

But he looked *really* good tonight, his usual rancher attire upgraded to include dark jeans and a shirt that looked more L.L.Bean than C.C. Filson, plus dress boots and a leather jacket.

Still, that was no reason for her blood to suddenly be humming in her veins.

And that was *before* he smiled at her.

As his lips curved, an unexpected warmth spread through her veins.

Or maybe she was having a hot flash.

Was twenty-nine too young for menopause?

Probably.

But she was reluctant to consider any other explanation for her physiological reaction to the rancher's presence.

"Hello, Ruby."

She managed to smile back. Even better, she didn't stammer as she replied, "Happy New Year, Julian."

"And to you," he said. "Though I'm sure it would be off to a better start if you hadn't had to work tonight."

"I didn't mind," she said. "It's not as if I had other plans, anyway."

"No other plans?" He sounded incredulous. "A beautiful woman like you? I find that hard to believe."

Beautiful? Did he really think so?

Or was he toying with her?

Either way, she felt her cheeks grow warm in response to his words.

"Trust me," she said. "There aren't too many men who want to ring in the New Year with a single mom and her four-year-old daughter."

"I think you'd be surprised," he said. "But speaking of—where is Emery tonight?"

She nodded toward the partially closed door behind her. "In the office."

"Eating caviar and sipping champagne?"

He was obviously teasing, but it had been so long since she'd exchanged playful banter with a handsome man that she'd evidently forgotten how.

"Sleeping."

Julian grinned at her lame response, anyway, and her knees melted.

Seriously, the man's smile should be registered as a lethal weapon.

Or maybe her visceral reaction was a sign that something was wrong with her.

This man was a friend—a *good* friend—of her ex-husband. And while that didn't necessarily make him her enemy, it certainly gave her cause to be wary.

Even if Julian had always been kind to her.

But she didn't think he was only being kind now.

In fact, it almost seemed as if he was flirting with her.

Or maybe that was wishful thinking on her part.

Because more than a year after her divorce—and three years after the breakdown of her marriage, she hadn't been on a single date. Which meant that she hadn't kissed a man—never mind anything more intimate than that—in more than three years.

In fact, it had been so long since she'd experienced anything like sexual desire, she'd been certain that her hormones had gone dormant, like flowering bulbs in the cold of winter. Except that winter had lasted three long years for Ruby, and though it was still winter now—and bitterly cold outside—those hormones seemed to be stirring to life again.

Her unexpected reaction to Julian's presence was so unnerving that she was almost relieved when her cellphone rang, intruding on their conversation.

She glanced at the unfamiliar number displayed on the screen.

It was just after midnight on New Year's Day, and as she'd exchanged text messages with her parents and each of her siblings earlier in the evening, she suspected this was probably a wrong number.

"Excuse me," she said to Julian.

"Of course."

She swiped to connect the call. "Hello?"

"Ruby McKinley?"

"Yes," she confirmed warily.

"It's Hazel Browning from Family Services."

The caller's identification only exacerbated Ruby's confusion.

Why would Family Services be calling her at this time of night?

Unless…

Her heart skipped a beat as cautious hope unfurled inside her.

"What can I do for you, Ms. Browning?"

"I'm hoping you can foster a baby boy."

Ruby was stunned.

Overjoyed.

And maybe just the teensiest bit apprehensive.

When she was interviewed after applying to be a foster parent, she'd been warned that she might never get a call. That her interest in being a foster parent was appreciated, but that single parents weren't able to provide the optimal environment for a child in need of a family.

She'd been disappointed, of course, but not really surprised.

If she'd had a choice, she wouldn't be raising her daughter as a single parent, either. But all things considered, it was preferable to raising Emery in a home where her dad's infidelities weren't a secret to anyone.

"Ms. McKinley? Are you there?"

"Yes," she said. "And yes, I'd be happy to take the baby, just tell me when."

"Now."

*"Now?"* she echoed, stunned.

"Or in about two hours," Ms. Browning clarified. "Which is how long it will take me to get the baby and all his stuff packed up and make the trip from Bronco."

"Two hours." She glanced at her watch.

"Is that a problem?"

"It's just that I'm at work right now. At the Tenacity Inn."

She heard papers rustling over the line before Ms. Browning spoke again. "There was nothing in your file indicating that you work nights."

"I don't usually," she explained. "I'm just covering for someone tonight."

"Well, you've got two hours to get someone to cover for you," Ms. Browning told her. "But if you don't think that's possible, I can call the next name on my list."

"No!" Ruby protested.

Her vehement response caused Chrissy Hastings-Parker to pause on her way past the desk.

"I'll figure something out," Ruby continued at a more normal volume. "Please don't call anyone else."

"Okay," Ms. Browning relented. And after verifying Ruby's address, she promised that she'd be on her way as soon as possible.

"Is everything okay?" Chrissy asked, when Ruby ended her call.

"That was Family Services."

Chrissy immediately went on the defensive. "Why would they be hassling you?" she demanded to know. "You're a wonderful mother to Emery."

"They're not hassling me," Ruby hastened to assure her friend. "I'm going to be a foster parent."

"Oh. Wow."

"Yeah, that's exactly how I'm feeling."

"So they have a child for you?"

She nodded. "A baby boy."

"I guess that's good news then," Chrissy said.

"Except that Ms. Browning is on her way from Bronco with the baby right now, and she expects me to be home to take custody of him in two hours and I'm scheduled to be here for another five."

"I can cover the desk for you," Julian said.

Ruby blinked.

In her excitement about the call, she'd forgotten that he was there.

*Why was he still there?*

"Thanks," she said. "But I can't just abandon my responsibilities to someone who has absolutely no hotel experience."

"How do you know I don't have any hotel experience?" he challenged.

"Just a wild guess," she said. "Am I wrong?"

"No," he admitted. "Unless checking in from the other side of the desk counts."

"It doesn't," she told him.

"But I have hotel experience," Chrissy chimed in. "I can hang out here until the day clerk arrives."

"I couldn't ask that of you," Ruby protested.

"You didn't ask, I offered," her friend reminded her. "And what other option do you have?"

"I was hoping Aihan might be willing to come in early."

"If she is and she can, great," Chrissy said. "If she isn't or can't, I'll be here until she shows up for her usual shift."

Ruby was torn. "I really would like to get Emery home and settled into bed before Ms. Browning arrives. And I should tidy up a little, because I'm sure she'll want to do a quick inspection of the house before she leaves the baby."

"So go," Chrissy urged. "And don't worry about the desk. I can't imagine anyone is going to be checking in during the wee hours of the morning of New Year's Day."

"I'm going," Ruby promised. "But before I do—would you know if there's anyone working in maintenance tonight?"

"What do you need?" Julian asked.

"If I've got time before the baby arrives, I might be able to put Emery's old crib together so he has somewhere to sleep."

"I can help with that," he said.

"Do you have more experience assembling cribs than you do behind a hotel desk?"

"As a matter of fact, I do. And while it's admittedly limited experience, it was assembling your daughter's crib."

"You put Emery's crib together?"

"Have you ever seen Owen assemble anything more complicated than an Ikea bookcase?"

"No," she admitted. "And even that wasn't completed without a lot of cursing."

"There's a surprise," Chrissy muttered under her breath.

"But I'm sure you have better things to be doing at—" she

glanced at the watch on her wrist "—half past midnight on New Year's Eve."

"Isn't it technically New Year's Day now?"

"I guess it is," she agreed.

"And no," he said. "I don't have anything better to be doing."

"How about sleeping?" she suggested. "Doesn't morning come early when you work on a ranch?"

"It does," he acknowledged. "But what kind of a cowboy would walk away from a woman in distress?"

"I'm not in distress," she felt compelled to point out.

Chrissy elbowed her in the ribs. "Ruby, the man's offering to do you a favor."

"And I appreciate it, but—"

"The correct response is, 'that would be helpful—thank you, Julian,'" her friend interjected.

Ruby felt her cheeks grow warm. "Is that the correct response?" she asked Julian.

He shrugged. "Only if you think it would be helpful."

"I do. I mean, it would. If you happen to have a screwdriver on you. My neighbor borrowed my toolbox on the weekend and hasn't yet returned it."

"I've got a whole set of screwdrivers in the toolbox in my truck."

"Then that would be helpful," she acknowledged. "Thank you, Julian."

He responded with a nod and a smile, and she nearly melted into a puddle at his feet.

"Now that wasn't so hard, was it?" Chrissy teased.

Ruby rolled her eyes at her friend, who grinned, unrepentant.

"I'll follow you home," Julian said.

Now Ruby nodded. "Okay. I just need a few minutes to pack up Emery and her things."

To her surprise, he followed her into the office and began

gathering up the books and toys that her daughter had left scattered around.

"Just dump everything into that bag," she said, gesturing to the bright pink-and-orange backpack that Emery insisted on taking with her everywhere.

While he did so, she wrestled her sleeping child into her puffy coat and snow boots.

Emery stirred as she tugged the second boot into place. "Mommy?"

"It's time to go home, Em."

Her daughter blinked sleepily. "Is it the New Year?"

"It is," she confirmed. "Happy New Year."

"Happy New Year," Emery echoed, yawning. Then, having caught sight of Julian, she said to him, "Who are you?"

"That's Mr. Sanchez," Ruby said.

"Julian," he chimed in.

But the little girl's interest in the stranger wasn't any match for her sleepiness, and her eyes drifted shut again.

Ruby retrieved her coat and purse from the rack by the door and buttoned herself up against the cold outside before reaching to lift her daughter into her arms.

"Let me carry her," Julian suggested.

"I can manage," Ruby assured him.

"I'm sure you can," he said. "But I'm offering to help."

Her friend's recent admonishment echoing in her head, she said, "That would be helpful—thank you, Julian."

He grinned and took the sleeping child from her arms.

Ruby picked up the backpack and her purse and led the way out of the office, pausing at the desk to thank Chrissy again and finagle her promise to call if she had any questions.

"The Honda SUV," she told Julian, gesturing with the key fob as they exited the building.

As she hit the unlock button, the lights flashed. She hurried to open the back door, so that he could put Emery in her car seat.

"I'm going to let you buckle her up. That way you know it's done right," Julian said, stepping back so that she could lean in to secure the five-point harness.

She started the engine and turned the defroster on high, then stepped out again with her snow brush in hand.

"Get in," Julian said, giving her a gentle nudge. "I'll clear the snow off."

"Shouldn't you be dealing with your own vehicle?"

"It had stopped snowing by the time I got here. My truck's fine."

With a shrug, she slid into the driver's seat and watched through the defrosting windshield as he brushed the snow away. When he was finished, he opened the passenger-side door and set the brush on the floor mat.

"I'll be right behind you," he promised.

"22 Pine Street," she said. "In case you lose me in traffic."

He chuckled at the unlikelihood of that happening and hurried to his truck.

She waited until she saw him pulling out of his spot, then made her way to the exit of the parking lot.

It was a short drive to her house from the inn—of course, most everything in Tenacity was a short drive from everything else—and less than ten minutes later, she was pulling into the driveway of the simple two-story Colonial that was now her home with Emery.

True to his word, Julian was right behind her.

She grabbed her purse and her daughter's backpack and unbuckled Emery's harness, then stepped back to allow him to pick up the still-sleeping child.

Her boot slipped on the bottom step and she wobbled a little. Even with his arms full of little girl, he managed to reach out and steady her.

"You alright?"

She nodded. "The steps are a little bit slippery. As soon as I get Emery settled in bed, I'll come back out to shovel them off. Or at least throw some salt down."

"You take care of your daughter," he said. "I'll take care of the steps."

She decided there was no point in arguing.

And why would she protest when the idea of venturing out into the cold again in the early hours of morning held little appeal?

He waited patiently in the foyer while she removed her boots and coat and put them away in the closet, and he continued to hold Emery while she took off her daughter's outerwear.

"S'eepy," the little girl said, her eyelids flickering.

"I know, baby," Ruby said, her voice a gentle whisper. "I'm going to take you up to bed right now."

"And I'll be back to deal with the crib as soon as I get those steps taken care of," Julian promised, matching her tone.

"You haven't asked where I keep my shovel," she noted.

"I don't need your shovel," he said. "I have one in the back of my truck. And a bag of salt, too."

"You must have been a Scout."

"I wasn't," he said. "But I did grow up in Montana, so I know the importance of traveling with the basic requirements for survival in winter."

"Then I'll let you get to it," she said. "Thank you."

But she stayed where she was for a few more seconds, watching as he walked out the door and thinking that it had been a long time since she'd had a man around her house—and certain she'd never had a man like Julian Sanchez.

# *Chapter Two*

He should have walked away.

Back at the inn, when Ruby excused herself to answer her phone, Julian should have turned around and gone back to the party.

But he'd been curious to know who might be calling her at such an hour, and that curiosity compelled him to linger.

Of course, being New Year's Eve, it could have been any number of people wanting to wish her a Happy New Year. A family member or friend. Possibly even a boyfriend.

Though he didn't think she had a boyfriend. He likely would have heard through the grapevine if she was dating anyone, but it wasn't outside the realm of possibility. Ruby McKinley was a beautiful woman and she'd been divorced for more than a year now.

The divorce—especially the reason for it—was further proof to Julian that Owen McKinley was a fool. Because he'd had an amazing woman like Ruby as his wife—and an adorable daughter like Emery—and he'd thrown it all away.

Of course, to hear Owen tell it, he was the injured party. He didn't want the divorce, but Ruby had kicked him out. The fact that he'd been cheating on her—and with more than one woman—wasn't any reason for her to abandon the vows he'd already broken. Besides, he'd continued to argue in his defense to his buddies at the Grizzly Bar, she'd let herself go when she got pregnant.

And then, after the baby was born, she barely had two minutes for him. Any time Emery made a sound, she jumped up to see what the kid needed. And the kid got a lot more boob time than he did. (Yes, those were Owen's actual words!)

Was it any wonder, he'd argued, that he'd found himself looking outside of the home for comfort and companionship?

As Julian sprinkled salt over the now cleared steps, the burn of his residual anger at his former friend ensured that he wasn't overly bothered by the cold temperature, despite the clouds that appeared with each breath he exhaled.

Sometimes he found himself wondering how he'd ever become friends with Owen McKinley. Of course, the absence of any kind of moral compass in his friend hadn't been as readily apparent to Julian back in high school, which was when Owen had sought him out. Even then, he'd known the most popular kid in school had ulterior motives for his apparent offer of friendship. But Julian hadn't cared, because hanging out with Owen immediately made him part of the "in" crowd, which afforded him a certain amount of deference and respect—and increased attention from the female element of the student body.

But while they'd both graduated from high school a lot of years earlier, it seemed that Owen had never really grown up. He still seemed to think he was the biggest man on campus and expected everyone else to defer to his wishes.

And why wouldn't he?

Owen had always gotten everything he wanted—including all the prettiest girls. Even Laura Bell, though Owen hadn't looked at Laura twice until Julian started dating her.

But that was a long time ago.

Water under the bridge—his mother would say.

After high school, Owen had immediately gone to work with his father at McKinley Insurance Brokers and Julian had been promoted to full-time ranch hand at Blue Sky Beef. With many of their former classmates off at college, Owen and Julian had spent a lot of their free time together.

Working a nine-to-five office job, Owen had a lot more free time, but Julian didn't envy him that. He'd much rather ride the range than sit behind a desk.

No, Julian didn't envy Owen at all until Ruby Jensen moved to town and Owen immediately moved in on her.

Less than six months later, they were engaged.

Six months after that, they were married.

Julian had stood up for his friend at the wedding, his heart aching with the certainty that Owen was marrying the woman meant for *him*.

Not that he would have ever let her know how he felt, because Owen had met her first, and there was no way he would ever make a move on his friend's girl.

But she wasn't Owen's girlfriend or fiancée or wife anymore.

She was his ex-wife.

A single woman.

And Julian had never stopped wanting her.

He'd spent a fair amount of time at their house when Owen and Ruby were married. After they separated, he had no excuse to stop by to see her or her daughter, who had taken hold of his heart as quickly and completely as Ruby had done.

But he'd knocked on her door once—after he'd heard that Owen was celebrating the finalization of his divorce in the Grizzly Bar—to make sure that she was okay.

She'd been wary.

Understandably, he supposed, as she'd only ever known him as Owen's friend.

But more than a year had passed since then—proof of which was most evident in her little girl. Emery had been a toddler the last time he saw her; now she was a preschooler. And every bit as irresistible as her mom.

He returned the shovel and salt to his truck and walked up to Ruby's front door with his toolbox in hand.

She opened the door before he had a chance to knock and offered him a smile.

And just like always, that smile landed like a fist to his solar plexus and stole all the air from his lungs.

She stepped back to allow him entry.

"Emery all tucked into bed?" he asked, when he'd managed to catch his breath and could speak again.

"Tucked in and fast asleep."

"To be a kid again," he mused.

"Tell me about it."

She hung up his coat while he took off his boots.

He noticed that she'd taken the time to change out of her work attire while he was outside, trading her black pants and blazer for a pair of navy leggings and a lighter blue sweater with a big sparkly snowflake on the front. Her hair was still loose, the blonde tresses spilling over her shoulders.

"Where's the crib?" he asked, picking up the toolbox again.

"Upstairs. In the spare bedroom."

She started up the stairs, and he followed—admiring the subtle sway of her hips and the shapely curve of her bottom.

"I almost got rid of it, when I was packing up for the move," she confided. "The way my marriage ended, I couldn't imagine that I'd ever have another child. But I guess I wasn't ready to give up the dream entirely, because I held on to all of Emy's baby furniture."

"A good thing," he noted.

She nodded.

"So this is where the baby's going to sleep?"

"Actually, it might be a better idea to put the crib in my room," she said. "I think he's only a few months old, which means he'll be up a few times in the night, and if he's all the way across the hall, he might wake up Emy before I can get to him."

"You *think* he's a few months old? They didn't give you any specific information about the child?"

She shrugged. "I was so surprised to get the call, I didn't think to ask."

"Why were you surprised?" he asked her now.

"When I was interviewed by Family Services, I was bluntly

advised not to get my hopes up, because single parents are always at the bottom of the list when it comes to placing a child."

"Apparently whoever told you that was wrong," he noted.

"More likely, being it was New Year's Eve, they couldn't get in touch with any of the other foster parents on the list and eventually made their way down to my name at the bottom."

"Even if that's true, I'd say the baby coming here lucked out."

"I hope he thinks so, too," she said, picking up one of the pieces of the disassembled crib leaning against one wall and carrying it across the hall.

He followed her with a couple more pieces, then made one more trip across the hall and he had all the pieces to begin assembly.

"Is it too much to hope that you have the instructions?" he asked.

She retrieved the manual from the other room. "Right here."

"Thanks."

She perched on the edge of the bed—neatly made with what looked like a handstitched quilt in various shades of blue and a couple of matching throw pillows—which wreaked havoc with his efforts to not think about the fact that he was in her bedroom, only a few feet away from the bed in which she slept.

*No good deed goes unpunished.*

He glanced at the instructions, wondering about the origin of the subtle scent that teased his nostrils. Her perfume? Shampoo? Or maybe the trio of chunky candles on her dresser?

"Can I help or do you want me out of your way?"

Ruby's question yanked his attention back to the task at hand.

"Actually, an extra set of hands would be good," he said. "You can hold the pieces in position while I secure them with the hardware."

"I can do that," she agreed. "Probably."

At his questioning look, she shrugged.

"Owen always said I was useless at household tasks."

"Well, your ex-husband always was an ass."

She seemed taken aback by his remark. "I thought you and Owen were good friends."

"We were," he said. "And then I realized that he was an ass. And an idiot."

A glimmer of amusement shone in the depths of her blue eyes. "And what made you come to that realization?"

"I saw the way he treated you."

The amusement vanished and she quickly looked away, a slight flush of color infusing her cheeks. "You know he cheated on me."

"I'm sorry. I shouldn't have said anything."

"No." She shook her head. "It's okay. I mean, it's *not* okay, but I'm sure, by the time I finally got around to kicking him out, everyone in town knew that he was tomcatting around."

"Which had absolutely nothing to do with you and everything to do with him," he assured her.

She laughed softly, though there was no humor in the sound. "It had everything to do with me, because I was his wife. If I'd been able to keep him satisfied, he wouldn't have gone looking elsewhere."

"I'm sure that's what he told you, to make you feel responsible," Julian said. "But you're smart enough to know it isn't true."

"So why do *you* think he cheated?" she asked him.

"Because marriage has specific rules, and Owen was never good at playing by the rules."

She breathed out a soft sigh. "I wish someone had told me that before we exchanged our vows."

"Would you have listened?"

"Probably not," she admitted.

"Because you were head over heels in love."

"Or thought I was, anyway," she said. "But even now, knowing what I know, I wouldn't go back in time and change anything if I could, because then I wouldn't have Emery."

"All things considered, you are a lucky woman," he said. "And she's a very lucky girl."

Ruby smiled again, a faint hint of blush coloring her cheeks.

For the next several minutes, their attention was focused on the assembly of the crib—which apparently didn't require his toolbox at all but only the Allen wrench that he'd found in the baggie with the dowel pins and screws and washers.

As he was attempting to tighten one of the screws, he drew in a breath and inhaled that tantalizing scent again. The Allen wrench slipped out of his grasp.

"I've got it," Ruby said, leaning forward to grab it.

As she did, her hair brushed against his cheek, tantalizing him with its silky texture and scent.

Yeah, it was definitely her shampoo—and how pathetic was it that he was turned on by whatever she used to wash her hair?

"Here you go." She held out her hand, showing him the tool.

His fingertips brushed against her open palm as he retrieved the wrench, and suddenly the air was crackling with electricity. He was pretty sure she felt it, too, because when Ruby's blue eyes lifted to his, he saw surprise and a hint of wariness in their depths.

"Thanks."

She cleared her throat. "No problem."

He set the last two screws in place.

"All done?" she asked.

"Now I have to go around and tighten all the connections, to ensure it stays together," he said. "But I can take it from here, if you've got other things to do."

"Oh. Okay. I'll, um, go get the crib sheet out of the dryer."

He was finishing up when Ruby returned with a pale yellow sheet dotted with Winnie the Pooh characters. He helped her cover the mattress, then dropped it into the crib.

A wistful smile curved her lips as she smoothed a hand over

an imaginary wrinkle in the crib sheet. "Emery's so big now, it's hard to believe that she used to sleep in this."

"How do you think she's going to feel about someone else sleeping in her crib?"

"She's going to be thrilled," Ruby said confidently. "Ever since she started preschool, she's been asking when she's going to get a baby brother or sister, like so many of her friends have."

"Kids never ask easy questions, do they?"

"Aside from 'what's for dinner?'—no," she agreed. "And although I tried to explain to her, when I filled out the application, that a foster sibling was like a temporary sibling, I'm not sure she's old enough to understand what 'temporary' means."

"You're worried that she's going to get too attached."

"I'm pretty confident we're both going to get too attached," she confided. "But even knowing that, I didn't withdraw my application, because I knew that if we were ever lucky enough to have a child placed with us, it would be because that child needed us—and I could never refuse a child in need."

"You're an amazing woman, Ruby McKinley."

She offered a small smile. "I don't know about that, but I do try to be a good example for my daughter. And—to tell you the truth—as excited as I am about this baby coming, I'm also a little apprehensive."

"Why would you be apprehensive?" he asked, surprised by her confession. "Emery is pretty solid proof that you know what you're doing when it comes to raising kids."

"Emery's a girl. This baby's a boy. I don't know anything about baby boys."

"I'm not sure there's very much difference when they're babies—they cry, they eat, they poop, they sleep. And the next day, they do it all again."

She laughed softly. "How much experience do you have with babies?"

"Not very much at all," he admitted. "Though I expect that

will change in the future, when my siblings get married and have kids."

"You don't plan to have any of your own?" Ruby asked.

He shrugged. "If my life had gone according to plan, I'd already be married with a couple rug rats running around the Sanchez ranch."

Her eyes widened with surprise. "You've got your own ranch now? When did that happen?"

"It hasn't happened yet," he admitted. "But I'm hopeful that things will start moving in that direction very soon."

"Well, good for you," she said. "And maybe the wife and kids will follow soon after?"

"Maybe."

They finally left the bedroom and made their way down the stairs again. She turned at the bottom, and he followed her into the kitchen. He glanced around, admiring the bright, cheery room with glossy white shaker-style cabinets, blue countertops and checkerboard blue-and-white tiles on the floor. He guessed that the wide window over the double sink looked into the backyard, though it was pitch dark outside now. The appliances looked moderately new, and the refrigerator even had a water and ice dispenser built into the door. To one side of the kitchen was a breakfast nook, with built-in seating and blue cushions that matched the countertop and floor tiles.

"Can I offer you something to drink?" Ruby asked him.

He was tempted by the offer—enticed by the opportunity to spend a little more time with her. But he thought they'd made some progress tonight in reestablishing a tentative bond of friendship and he didn't want to push for too much too soon.

He understood that his connection to Owen gave her cause to be wary, so he was determined to take things slow, to ensure that she knew his interest in her had absolutely nothing to do with her ex-husband and everything to do with the fact that, even after watching her exchange vows with said ex-husband, he'd never quite managed to shake the feeling that she was meant to be with *him*. Though he suspected it was going to take some time to convince her of the fact.

"Thanks," he said. "But I should be heading out. You don't want to have to explain the presence of a strange man in your home when the lady from Family Services arrives."

"You're not all *that* strange," she said.

She was teasing—a sign, he hoped, that she was already starting to feel more comfortable around him.

"Rain check?" he asked.

"Of course."

He headed out.

It was almost 3:00 a.m. before Hazel Browning arrived with the baby, and while Ruby could have—and should have—napped while she waited, she was too excited to sleep. And too worried that the social worker's inspection of her home might find it lacking in some way, so Ruby spent the time polishing away every last speck of dirt and sweeping up every hidden dust bunny to ensure Ms. Browning would have no reason not to leave the baby with her.

But notwithstanding her excitement over their imminent arrival, as she'd wiped fingerprint smudges off the refrigerator and polished the mirror in the bathroom, Ruby had found her thoughts wandering in an unexpected direction—to Julian Sanchez!

She didn't know what had compelled him to offer his help with the crib, but she was sincerely grateful—and a little bit uneasy to acknowledge, if only to herself, her response to his nearness.

It had been so long since she'd felt the first stirrings of attraction to a man, and the fact that it was Julian—a friend of her ex-husband's—was more than a little unnerving.

The tap on the door jolted her back to the present and caused her heart to leap inside her chest.

They were here.

*He* was here.

She hurried to open the door.

"Take him," Hazel Browning said, shoving the infant car seat at Ruby. "I've got a bunch of other stuff to bring in."

Before Ruby had a chance to respond, the social worker was gone again.

"Okay," she said, lifting the car seat higher to peer at the baby securely buckled inside. "I guess it's just you and me for the moment."

His big blue eyes, with ridiculously long lashes, stared back at her. His chubby cheeks were pink, no doubt from his brief exposure to the cold, and his expression was solemn.

"Well, having your life upended is serious business," she noted, moving into the living room to set the carrier on the coffee table. "I've had some experience with that, so I can empathize." She knelt in front of the baby to unfasten his harness. "But wherever you came from, you're going to be staying here with me and my daughter, Emery, for a little while. Or maybe a long while. I really have no idea at this point, but I promise that we will take very good care of you for as long as you're with us."

Suddenly and unexpectedly, the baby's adorable Cupid's bow mouth curved, and Ruby's heart completely melted.

The same thing had happened the first time she'd felt movement inside her womb when she was pregnant with Emery. In that moment, she'd known that she would do anything to protect her child. And she felt exactly the same about this one.

It didn't matter that she didn't share the same biological connection to him. It only mattered that he was a child—an innocent, helpless baby—who needed someone in his corner.

"My name's Ruby." She lifted him out of the seat and snuggled him close to her body, breathing in his sweet baby scent. "And hopefully I'll learn your name when Ms. Browning comes back."

"It's Jay," the social worker said, returning with a case of formula balanced on top of a box of diapers in one arm and a clear garbage bag full of baby clothes clutched in her other fist.

"Jay," Ruby echoed. "Is that short for Jason? Or Jack? Or something else?"

"Nope, it's just the long version of the letter." She deposited the items she carried on the floor inside the living room. "Dottie named him."

"Dottie?"

"His first foster mom," Hazel explained. "He didn't have a name when he came to us, so Dottie suggested J—because *j* is the tenth letter of the alphabet and he was her tenth foster child."

"Why did Dottie give him up?" Ruby asked curiously.

"She didn't give him up—she had a heart attack."

She was immediately concerned. "Is she going to be okay?"

"The doctors expect her to make a full recovery, eventually. But right now, she's obviously unable to care for a baby, which is why we called you."

"Or several other applicants before me," Ruby guessed.

"It wouldn't have been my first choice to drive a hundred miles to a new placement," the social worker acknowledged. "But I wouldn't be here if I didn't trust you can provide the care he needs."

"I can. And I will," Ruby promised, already fiercely protective of the baby in her arms.

Hazel nodded. "I'm just going to take a quick look around, and then I'll leave the two of you to get better acquainted."

"Of course," Ruby agreed, understanding that it was the only acceptable answer. "Although I'd think this little guy is probably more interested in sleep than anything else after the busy day he's had."

"You'd think," the other woman agreed.

They were both wrong.

# *Chapter Three*

Ruby had been right about morning coming early for a rancher. And for some reason, bitterly cold winter mornings seemed to come even earlier than most.

As Julian traversed the open fields on the ATV, icy snowflakes stinging his cheeks, he considered—not for the first time—why he wasn't moving south to pursue his goal of owning his own ranch. Texas, for example, was renowned for its cattle—and a much more hospitable climate.

But the answer to that question was simple: he couldn't leave Montana because his family was here. His parents and his siblings were the reason his boots remained firmly planted in northwestern soil.

Well, his family *and* Ruby.

He was, of course, familiar with all the Ten Commandments, and of the fact that he was guilty of coveting his friend's wife—even if he'd never acted on those feelings.

The first time he met Ruby, she was already Owen's girlfriend. But his friend had never been the type to date any one woman for long, and he'd felt confident that Ruby would soon be Owen's *ex*-girlfriend.

Six months later he'd been proven wrong when, instead of ending his relationship with Ruby, Owen put a ring on her finger.

Julian had toasted the happy couple at their engagement party—because what else was he going to do? And when they set a date for their wedding, he felt certain that their impending nuptials were the incentive he needed to finally get over his secret crush on his friend's bride-to-be.

As he watched them exchange their vows, he sincerely hoped their marriage would last, because it was obvious that Owen made Ruby happy, and he wanted nothing more than for her to be happy.

And she was—for a while.

During the course of their short-lived marriage, Julian had been a regular visitor to their home, because he believed that spending time with Owen and Ruby—painful though it might be—would force him to accept that any illusions he had about a future with his friend's wife weren't anything more than that. And when Emery was born, he'd immediately become "Uncle" Julian to their infant daughter.

But Ruby was no longer Owen's wife, and Julian no longer believed that his feelings for her would fade.

In fact, spending just a few hours with Ruby the previous evening had proved the exact opposite. And then, when he'd finally gone back to the house he rented for its proximity to Blue Sky rather than its dubious charm and crawled into his empty bed, he'd dreamed about her.

Yeah, there was no doubt that he had it bad.

The question now was—what was he going to do about it?

It was, he decided, a question better pondered indoors, because the air temperature was cold enough to freeze the balls off a pool table.

His breath made puffy clouds in the air as he broke up the ice that had formed on the surface of the watering troughs overnight. Having completed his task, he climbed onto the ATV again and turned back to the barn.

He didn't think he'd mind the bone-chilling cold so much if he was ensuring the water supply for his own cattle, if the fields in which they foraged were his own land. But the fact that he was out here while Colin Hanrahan was most likely cozy and warm in his big fancy house with his wife and kids scraped like the raw wind.

*Algún día.*

*Someday.*

Someday he'd have his own spread, his own home, his own family.

But he'd been saving for as long as he'd been working and had started to question whether his "someday" would ever come.

Spending time with Ruby the previous evening had renewed his commitment to his goals and inspired him to turn his dreams into reality. Not "someday" but "soon."

And Ruby was an essential element of that dream. Not only because she was smart and sexy, but because she was one of the warmest and kindest people he'd ever met. Despite having her hands full with her house and her job and her own daughter, she was nevertheless willing to open her heart and her home to a child who needed love and shelter.

Julian could only hope that he'd be able to convince her to open her heart to him, too.

Until then, he'd be satisfied with her opening her door again.

Ruby lifted the pot of freshly brewed coffee to refill her mug, desperate for the caffeine to kick her brain into gear.

"I wanna juice box, Mommy."

Her daughter's impatient demand yanked Ruby's attention back to the present.

"We don't have any juice boxes," she said, pouring milk into a cup.

Emery looked at the cup with suspicion when Ruby put it on the table beside her plate of cheesy scrambled eggs.

"Where's your breakfast, Mommy?"

She held up her mug of coffee. "Right here."

"Mimi says breakfast is the most 'portant meal of the day."

"Mimi" was Emery's name for her paternal grandmother, and while Ruby might despair that her ex-husband was the very definition of an absentee father, she found some solace in the fact that Owen's parents were wonderful grandparents.

"Mimi's right," Ruby said. "Which is why you need to eat up all of your eggs."

In fact, the eggs she'd made for her daughter were actually a second breakfast, aka lunch, as she'd given Emery a bowl of cold cereal when she first woke up. But the little girl considered eggs breakfast, whether she was eating them for breakfast, lunch or dinner, and Ruby didn't bother to dispute her characterization now.

"I said I wanted waffles for breakfast."

"And I heard you, but we don't have any waffles."

Another item on her grocery list.

"Mimi makes waffles in a pan, not the toaster."

"That's because Mimi has more than two minutes to put breakfast in front of you before she has to hustle you out the door to preschool and herself to work."

Emy poked at her eggs with her fork. "Do I go to preschool today?"

"No. We're both on holidays until Monday."

"Is Jay on holidays, too?"

Emery had been overjoyed to see the baby sleeping in the crib in her mom's bedroom when she woke up that morning and had been full of questions about him ever since.

"He is," Ruby confirmed.

"Is that why he's still sleeping?"

"He's still sleeping because he was up very late last night."

"Past his bedtime?"

"Way past his bedtime—and mine, too."

"When is he gonna wake up?"

"Probably when he gets hungry."

"I wanna play with him."

"I know you do," Ruby said. "But Jay is just a baby, and babies can't really do much."

"What can they do?" Emy pressed.

"They cry, they eat, they poop and they sleep," she said, echoing what Julian had said the night before.

Emy giggled. "I can do all those things, too."

"That's true. But you can also walk and talk and eat scrambled eggs with a fork."

The little girl dutifully moved a forkful of eggs from her plate to her mouth. "What does Jay eat?"

"Right now, he only has formula."

"What's that?"

"It's a special milk that gives him all the good stuff he needs to grow big and strong."

"Can he have cookies with his milk?"

"No. He definitely cannot have cookies," she said firmly.

"But *I* can have cookies," Emy said, just in case her mom needed a reminder. "Because I'm a big girl."

"You are a big girl," Ruby agreed. "But you're not going to grow any bigger if you don't eat your breakfast."

"I want juice."

"You have milk," she told her daughter.

"I want juice," Emery said again.

"We'll get more juice boxes tomorrow, when the grocery store is open. Today, you'll have to drink milk."

Emery responded to that by pushing her cup off the table.

Thankfully, it was a sippy cup with a no-spill lid.

"And now you don't have anything to drink," Ruby said, picking up the cup and setting it on the counter.

"Drink! Drink!" The little girl punctuated her demand by banging her fork on the table.

"Emery, please be quiet so you don't wake the baby."

But the caution came too late and was immediately followed by the sound of a muffled cry through the baby monitor.

And then her phone rang.

"Finish your breakfast," she instructed her daughter, grabbing her phone as she headed toward the stairs.

Could it be Ms. Browning checking up on her already?

She didn't recognize the number—and it obviously wasn't anyone in her list of contacts or the name would have shown up on the screen—and answered warily.

"Hello?"

"Good morning, Ruby."

A warm and distinctly masculine voice.

Definitely *not* Ms. Browning.

And while there was something familiar about the voice, she couldn't immediately put a name to it, though the sudden warmth that flooded her veins should have been a clue.

She glanced at her watch. "It's after noon."

"It is," he acknowledged. "But considering your late night, I thought you might have slept in today."

Now the pieces clicked together. "Julian?"

"I probably should have led with that," he noted.

"Or you could just tell me why you're calling," she said, wedging the phone between her ear and her shoulder so her hands were free to pick up the baby.

"I just wanted to make sure the crib held up through the night."

"I never had any doubt that it would." She nuzzled Jay's cheek, and he responded with a gummy smile. "And the baby slept like a baby—when he finally got to sleep."

She carried the infant down the stairs to check on her daughter, who was finger-painting the table with the remnants of her scrambled egg.

Because that's what happened when you left a four-year-old unattended for thirty seconds.

She bit back a sigh as she settled Jay in his reclining high chair and secured the belt around his middle.

"Do you need me to bring coffee?" Julian asked.

She moistened the cloth under the faucet. "Actually, I'm only about halfway through the pot that I made this morning."

She usually only made half a pot, but today she'd filled the water reservoir to the max, then, after measuring the grounds into the filter, added an extra scoop.

"In that case, maybe I could cash in that rain check you gave me last night?"

"You want to come over? For coffee?"

Butterflies fluttered in her tummy.

"Only if I wouldn't be interrupting anything," he said.

"Yes," she said. "I mean, no. You wouldn't be interrupting. I'll even put on a fresh pot."

"There's no need for that," he said.

"I don't mind," she assured him. "But if you want cream, you're out of luck."

"Do you usually use cream?"

"Yeah, but I didn't make it to the grocery store yesterday."

"I want juice, Mommy."

She pulled the phone away from her face before responding to her daughter. "I told you, we'll get juice boxes when the grocery store opens tomorrow."

Emery kicked the leg of the table. "I want juice *now*."

This time Ruby didn't quite manage to hold back the sigh.

"I can be there around two, if that's okay," Julian said.

"Two o'clock is good," she said, relieved that she'd have time to put on something more suitable for company than the oversize nightshirt with a cartoon bear yawning on the front with the words "Mornings Are Unbearable" beneath his bunny-slipper-clad feet.

Julian had planned to play it cool.

Considering how reluctant Ruby had been to accept his offer of help the night before, he'd decided to give her some time before he made their paths cross again. But after he'd finished his morning chores on the ranch, he decided that he'd waited long enough.

After all, it was a new year, and he had goals.

Ruby opened the door in response to his knock, a weary smile on her face and a little girl cautiously peeking out from behind her.

"I heard someone say they wanted juice boxes," he said, holding up a bag from the local convenience store.

"Me! Me!" Emery said, her initial shyness pushed aside by her excitement.

"What do you like—apple or grape?"

"I like apple *and* grape."

"Then I guess it's a good thing I got some of each," he said.

Ruby eyed him warily. "How did you know?"

"I heard Emery when we were on the phone. And I saw the grocery list on your fridge last night, so I knew what kind to buy."

"Well, aren't you observant," she mused. "And thoughtful."

"I brought something for you, too," he said.

"What's that?"

"Cream for your coffee. And doughnuts—just because."

"And there goes my New Year's resolution to cut out junk food," she said.

"Do you want me to take them back?"

She snatched the bag out of his hand. "Don't even think about it."

He chuckled as he followed her into the kitchen, where the coffee was just finishing brewing.

"I told you not to worry about making a fresh pot."

"No way I was going to serve stale coffee to company."

"Am I company?"

She looked at him warily, as if it was a trick question. "Aren't you company?"

He shrugged. "I thought—I hoped—we were friends."

She didn't seem to know how to respond to that, so he granted her a reprieve by turning his attention to the wide-eyed baby reclined in the high chair.

"So you're the little guy that all the big fuss is about, huh?"

"He can't talk to you, cuz he's just a baby," Emery said, climbing into her booster seat at the table.

"Is that why?"

She nodded. "I was hoping we'd get a girl baby, but we got a boy baby instead."

"Does the boy baby have a name?" he asked her.

"Jay," she said. "It's a name *and* a letter in the alphabet. Just like my name."

"I thought your name was Emery."

She nodded. "But sometimes Mommy calls me 'Em.'"

"And sometimes Emy," Ruby chimed in.

"And sometimes Emery Rose McKinley." She fisted her hands on her hips, as if imitating her mother, and deepened her voice as she continued, "'I said *right now*, Emery Rose McKinley.'"

Julian covered his laugh with a fake cough.

"Thank you for that, Emery Rose McKinley," Ruby said dryly.

The little girl responded with a grin.

Ruby finished unpacking the contents of the grocery bag, then poked a straw in the top of one of the juice boxes and set it on the table in front of her daughter.

"Thank you," she said politely.

"You should say *thank you* to Mr. Sanchez," Ruby told her. "He brought the juice boxes for you."

"Julian," he corrected her again.

"Maybe Uncle Julian?" she suggested, as an alternative.

He nodded, pleased to have his honorary title restored.

"Thank you, Unca Julian," Emery dutifully intoned.

"You're welcome, Emery."

Ruby filled the two mugs with fresh coffee and handed him one.

"Thank you."

"You're welcome, Unca Julian," she said, with a smile that told him she was teasing.

Ruby added a splash of cream to her coffee, then arranged some of the doughnuts on a plate before carrying both to the table.

She took the seat across from him and beside her daughter, who was studying Julian as she sipped her juice. The baby, he noted, had tracked Ruby's movements, and he kicked his legs when she sat down near him.

Ruby obviously noticed, too, because she smiled and tweaked his toes. The infant responded with another kick and a toothless grin.

Julian sipped his coffee. "Did you say the social worker brought the baby from Bronco?"

"Yeah." Ruby tapped a doughnut on the edge of the plate to knock off the excess sugar. "Why?"

"I wonder if Jay might be the baby that Marisa told us about—the one who was found at the church when she was in Bronco working on the holiday pageant."

"Ms. Browning did say that the baby had been abandoned at a church," Ruby acknowledged, offering the doughnut to Emery.

The little girl eagerly accepted the treat and immediately took a big bite.

"It's hard to believe that a mother could just walk away from her newborn baby," he mused.

"You're assuming it was the mother who abandoned him," Ruby pointed out.

"Who else could it be?"

"That's a good question," she admitted. "And one with countless possible answers. The father, a boyfriend of the mom who wasn't the father, a grandparent of the child, a neighbor or friend who believed the child wasn't being adequately cared for—or someone else with less benevolent motives."

"You seem to have given the matter some thought," he noted.

"Because my initial reaction was the same as yours," she admitted. "But the fact is, no one knows. And until the mom or dad or another family member is found, we won't."

"Can I go play now, Mommy?"

"Not until we clean all that powdered sugar off your hands and face," Ruby said, pushing away from the table.

The little girl dutifully stayed put while her mom moistened a washcloth and cleaned her up.

"And now I'm wondering about something else," Julian said, after Emery had scampered off.

"What's that?"

"Why a woman—a single mom—who works full-time and has a busy child of her own to care for would apply to be a foster parent."

Ruby brought the coffeepot to the table to refill both their mugs. "I've always wanted a big family, so that Emy could grow up with brothers and sisters, like I did. But my marriage falling apart kind of nixed that plan."

After setting the pot back on the warmer, she returned to her seat at the table. "And then I read an article about fostering and it seemed like a good opportunity to give a home to a child who needed one and give my daughter the experience of being a sibling."

He was hesitant to ask the next question but forged ahead, anyway. "You don't think you'll ever marry again?"

"I haven't completely written off the possibility," she said. "But I don't exactly have men lining up at the door to go out with me."

"Does that mean you're not seeing anyone right now?"

She shook her head. "I haven't been on a date since…well, it's been a long time."

Julian wasn't really surprised by the admission, because he imagined being a single mom took precedence over all else. But this confirmation that she was unattached threatened to wreak havoc on his efforts to keep his distance from his ex-best friend's ex.

"Look, Mommy! It's snowing."

Ruby turned her head to glance out the window behind her and confirm her daughter's proclamation.

"Santa brought Em a new sled for Christmas," she told Julian, explaining her daughter's enthusiasm for the weather. "Now every time it snows, she wants to go tobogganing."

"What was Santa thinking?" he asked, tongue-in-cheek.

"Obviously he wasn't thinking that Emery's mom would have to trek over to the park after every snowfall—or that winter seems to last forever in Montana."

Julian chuckled.

Ruby lifted her mug to her lips, attempting to hide her yawn.

"You're tired," he realized, and immediately felt guilty that he'd invited himself over when he knew she'd had a late night the night before.

"It was almost 3:00 a.m. before Ms. Browning arrived," she confided.

He winced. "That late?"

She nodded. "And after Jay slept in the car the whole way from Bronco, he was wide awake. Every time I tried to put him down, he started to cry, which led to me picking him up again so that he wouldn't wake up Emery. So we spent the next few hours playing pat-a-cake and peek-a-boo. I swear the sun was starting to rise by the time he finally fell asleep, which meant that I could finally get some sleep, too.

"And then Emery was awake about two hours later—hence the need for coffee," she said, lifting her mug to her lips. "Lots of coffee."

"I think what you need more than coffee is a nap."

"Unfortunately, that's not going to happen."

"Why not?"

"Because it's time to feed the baby again." She rose from the table to mix the powdered formula.

"And after you feed him, he's probably going to have a nap, right?" he asked, looking at the baby, whose eyes were already starting to look heavy.

"The odds are very good," she confirmed, pouring the formula into a bottle.

"So why don't you sleep when he does?"

"Because I've got company. And a four-year-old."

"I'm not company, I'm a friend."

She nodded, acknowledging the point. "But my daughter still needs adult supervision, and I suspect that she's only going to be distracted from the idea of tobogganing by the promise of fort building in the living room."

"Well then, this is your lucky day," Julian said. "Because it just so happens that I have serious fort-building skills."

# Chapter Four

Ruby was exhausted enough to let Julian put his fort-building skills to the test. And apparently Emery was satisfied with his efforts, because she didn't interrupt her mom's nap even once. It was only when Jay started to stir in his crib, waking from his slumber, that Ruby was awakened from hers.

A quick glance at the clock on her bedside table told her that she'd been out for almost two hours—and if she didn't exactly feel well-rested, she at least felt a lot better than she had when she'd laid down.

And a little unnerved, because her sleep had not been without dreams, and those dreams had starred Julian! She didn't clearly remember the details, and maybe that was a good thing, because the bits that she did remember—warm lips moving against hers, callused hands exploring her naked skin—made her feel hot and achy all over.

Pushing those alluring memories aside along with the covers, Ruby rose to deal with the baby. After changing Jay's diaper, she carried him downstairs, where she found her daughter set up at the kitchen table with a coloring book and crayons and Julian standing in front of the stove.

"I think I must still be dreaming," Ruby mused aloud from the doorway. And this image was almost as tantalizing as her erotic dream.

Julian glanced over his shoulder and smiled at her. "How are you feeling?"

"So much better."

"Hungry?"

"A little." She dropped a kiss on her daughter's head before settling Jay into his high chair so that she could make him a bottle.

She blinked when Julian handed her a bottle of formula.

"I mixed it up when I heard you moving around upstairs."

"Oh. Um. Thank you."

He looked amused. "Are you surprised that I was able to read the can and follow the instructions?"

She flushed. "No. Of course not. I'm just…surprised…that you would think to do so."

Because her ex-husband certainly wouldn't have.

Even when she'd asked for his help, Owen often feigned ignorance to get out of lending a hand with childcare duties.

"And you're making dinner, too," she realized.

"I hope you don't mind that I made myself at home in your kitchen."

"I definitely don't mind," she said. "But I really didn't expect this."

"I had an ulterior motive," Julian said, with a playful wink. "Which was hoping that you'd invite me to stay and have dinner with you."

"Consider yourself invited," she said, moving closer to look at the contents of the pan.

"It's sweet-and-spicy chicken. One of my mom's recipes."

"It looks—and smells—delicious," she said. "But I don't know if Emery will eat it."

"I wondered about that myself," he told her. "Which is why I made chicken fingers for her."

"I didn't think I had any chicken fingers." It was yet one more thing on her grocery list.

"You didn't, but you had chicken."

"Are you telling me that you *made* chicken fingers?"

"Actually, Emery and I made them together."

In response to her name, the little girl looked up and grinned.

"How did she help?" Ruby wondered.

"She crushed the cornflakes and cracked the eggs."

Ruby settled into a chair beside her daughter and tucked the baby into the crook of her arm before offering him the bottle. "Emery does like to break things."

Julian chuckled. "She was very helpful."

"Still, I can't believe you made chicken fingers."

"I would have thought you'd be more impressed with the sweet-and-spicy chicken."

"I am," she assured him. "And even more impressed that you were able to find all the ingredients you needed in my poorly stocked kitchen."

He chuckled. "This is where I have to confess that I made a couple of substitutions, but it looks pretty much as it should."

Emery abandoned her coloring and slid out of her seat to move closer to her mom.

"Can I help, Mommy?"

"Sure you can help," Ruby agreed, guiding her daughter's hand to the bottle. "Just make sure you hold it at an angle—like this—so he's sucking down formula and not air."

"Why not air?"

"Because air will make his tummy hurt." She brushed her free hand over the little girl's hair. "And you know how uncomfortable it is when your tummy hurts, don't you?"

Emery nodded, her attention focused on the baby.

Ruby was happy to see her helping out, because giving Emery the experience of being a big sister was one of her goals when she signed up to become a foster parent.

"Dinner will be ready in twenty minutes if I put the rice on now," Julian said. "Does that work?"

"That's perfect," Ruby agreed, ignoring the pang of regret that tugged at her heart.

This was what she'd imagined married life would be like: a couple working together to take care of their children and put a meal on the table. And though she and Julian weren't a couple and Emery and Jay weren't his responsibility, sometimes it was nice to dream.

\* \* \*

Julian felt pretty good about the fact that he'd managed to put a meal together for Ruby and Emery—especially considering the limited contents of the refrigerator and pantry. Or he did, until Emery looked at the chicken fingers and rice on her plate and asked, "Where's the veggies?"

"Um…" He glanced at Ruby questioningly.

"We have a rule about including veggies with dinner," she explained.

"Well, the breading on the chicken fingers is made from corn-flakes," he reminded the little girl. "And cornflakes are made from corn."

"Does that count?" Emery asked her mom.

"We'll let it count tonight," she said. "But there are carrot sticks and cucumber wheels in the fridge, if you want some."

Emy shook her head.

"There are peppers in the sweet-and-spicy chicken," he told Ruby.

"I'm not judging," she assured him. "But I am eager to try it."

He set a plate in front of her and took a seat across the table. The baby, his belly already full, was strapped into something that Ruby called a bouncy chair, contentedly looking at the soft toys dangling from the handle.

"What's that?" Emy asked, eyeing the contents of her mother's plate with interest.

"This is chicken and rice, too," she said. "Just cooked a different way. Do you want to try it?"

The little girl considered a minute, then nodded.

Ruby transferred a piece of chicken, a chunk of pepper and a little bit of sauce to her daughter's plate.

Emery stabbed the chicken with her fork.

"It might be hot," Ruby cautioned.

Em puckered up and huffed out a breath as if she was blowing out birthday candles.

After a few more huffs, Ruby said, "I think it's probably good now."

She opened her mouth and tentatively bit into the chicken. Almost immediately, her face scrunched up and she dropped her fork. "Yuck."

"That's not going to translate to a very good Yelp review," Julian remarked.

"No," Ruby agreed, digging into her meal again. "But I would rate your sweet-and-spicy chicken five stars."

"Only because you haven't had my mother's tamales," he said. "Now those are worthy of five stars."

"I'm still sticking with my five-star rating for this chicken."

"I guess my mother should get credit for it, too," he acknowledged. "She made sure that each of her kids was capable of putting a meal on the table. Because as much as she's always on me about finding a nice girl to settle down with, she does not believe it's a woman's job to cook for her husband. Or make his bed or do his laundry."

Ruby smiled at that. "I think I'd like your mom."

"I know she likes you."

She seemed taken aback by his response. "When did I ever meet your mom?"

"Both my parents were at your wedding," he said. "And now I'm wishing I'd kept my mouth shut."

"Why?"

"I don't want to be responsible for stirring up unhappy memories."

"My memories of that day are happy," she told him. "But I met and talked to so many people, they all blurred together in my mind."

"That's understandable," he said. "At least I know you liked their wedding gift."

"All done, Mommy," Emery said, pushing her mostly empty plate toward her mom. "Can I watch TV?"

Ruby pushed away from the table to get a cloth to wipe her daughter's face and hands. "What do you want to watch?"

"*Paw Patrol*!"

"One episode," her mom said.

Emery skipped out of the kitchen.

"Now might be a good time to tell you that we didn't break down the fort before we decided to make dinner," Julian said.

"I saw it when I came down the stairs," Ruby admitted. "I thought maybe you'd deliberately left it intact to show off your fort-building skills."

"That might have been a factor."

She picked up her fork again. "Anyway, back to the wedding gift from your parents—do you mean the hand-painted mugs from Mexico?"

He nodded. "They were made in the mountains of Michoacán, where my mom's family came from. The capulin design celebrates the Mexican cherry flower."

"I love those mugs. In fact, I specifically asked for them when the lawyers were divvying up our possessions during the divorce negotiations."

"Well, they certainly go well with your kitchen."

"When I was looking to buy a new house—for me and Emery—this kitchen tipped the scales for me."

"It is a nice kitchen."

"It's blue."

"More white than blue, but okay," Julian said.

"The house on Mountain Drive—the house that Owen picked out for us—was beige. Inside and out. I hated that house."

"It's simple enough to paint over beige."

"Owen wouldn't let me paint. He wouldn't let me put colorful throw cushions on the beige sofa. I bought a glass bowl for the coffee table—blown glass in shades of red and orange and gold. He threw it out."

"I didn't know he had an aversion to color."

"I didn't, either, until we were married."

"He must have really hated those coffee mugs," Julian mused.

"So much so that they were tucked away in the back of the cupboard above the refrigerator," she confided. "And when I stood in the middle of this kitchen, I actually thought 'my mugs belong here.' And that's when I knew that Emy and I belonged here, too."

"And if they'd given you orange mugs instead of blue?"

She pushed away from the table to carry their empty plates to the counter. "I would have bought the house on Juniper Lane."

He chuckled and followed her to the kitchen.

"Looks like you've got leftovers for lunch tomorrow," Julian noted, as she dished the remaining rice and chicken into a plastic container.

"Lucky me," she said. "Em might be happy with PB&J every day, but I like some variety. And I really like this chicken."

"I'd give you the recipe," he said. "But I'm afraid that you'll be a lot less impressed when you realize how simple it is to make."

"You made dinner for me—I will forever be impressed by that," she promised.

He put the stopper in the bottom of the sink and turned on the faucet.

"What are you doing?" Ruby demanded.

"I was just going to wash the pots and pans."

"No, you are *not*," she said. "You cooked. I'll deal with the cleanup."

"Who does the dishes after you cook?" he asked her.

Her cheeks colored. "That's different."

"Why?" he challenged.

"Because it's my house. My child. My responsibility."

"You don't ever let anyone help you out?"

"Of course, I do." She squirted liquid soap into the stream of water. "But you've already helped a lot. After a two-hour nap and that delicious meal, I almost feel human again."

"I'm glad." He frowned as she lowered the stack of plates into the sudsy water. "Why don't you use the dishwasher?"

"It's on the fritz," she admitted.

"Is that the technical term?" he couldn't resist teasing.

She responded with a smile and a shrug. "I don't actually know the technical term for the fact that water pours into the adjacent cupboard."

"Sounds like a connection issue," he said. "Or possibly a damaged hose."

"Either way, to me it sounded like a costly and unnecessary repair," she countered. "And I really don't mind doing a few dishes every night."

"I could take a look," he said.

"Or you could sit down and relax," she suggested. "I think you've earned it."

He sat, because it seemed important to her.

As soon as he did, the baby started to fuss.

Ruby sighed and lifted her hands out of the soapy water.

"I've got him," Julian said, lifting the bouncy chair up to set it on the table in front of him.

The baby looked at him for a minute with big, solemn eyes—and then rewarded him with a smile.

"This is a seriously cute kid," he remarked.

"You're telling me," she agreed, as she resumed washing.

"I bet he's already got you wrapped around his little finger."

"More tightly than he's holding on to yours right now," she admitted.

"So what are you going to do with this little guy when you have to work?" Julian asked.

"Thankfully, I don't work again until Monday," she told him. "I booked holidays so that I could spend more time with Emery during her school break."

"I can't believe she's in school."

"Preschool," she clarified.

"Still." It was hard to believe that the child he'd known since she was younger than this one was already spending some of her days in a classroom.

Ruby nodded. "They grow up fast."

"Too fast." Or maybe it wasn't too fast and just that he'd stayed away for too long. And though he wasn't entirely certain he should be here right now, when he saw Ruby working at the inn the night before, he knew he couldn't stay away any longer.

"As for Jay," Ruby continued, "I guess I'll take him to work with me."

"Your boss won't mind?" he asked.

"It's what I used to do with Emery, before I got her into Little Cowpokes Daycare, so I don't anticipate there being a problem." She glanced at the clock on the wall again as she rinsed the last plate before setting it in the drying rack. "But speaking of Emery, I need to get her ready for bed."

"Is that your polite way of asking me to leave so that you can carry on with your usual routines?"

"I don't mind if you stay," she said, drying her hands on a towel. "I mean, if you want to stay."

He did want to stay. Maybe too much.

Now his gaze shifted to the clock. "I've actually got plans with my brother tonight," he admitted, sincerely regretful. "But I can hang out with this little guy while you get Emery settled."

"That would be great." She touched a hand to his arm. "Thank you."

He knew the touch had been nothing more than a casual gesture meant to reinforce her words, but something electric passed between them during that brief contact.

Something that caused her eyes to widen as they locked with his, for just a moment, as the air fairly crackled with static.

Then the baby blew a raspberry, and the moment was over.

"You're cute," Julian said to the baby, when Ruby was gone. "But your timing sucks."

The little guy looked at him, all wide-eyed innocence—and then his mouth curved.

And Julian couldn't help but smile back.

# *Chapter Five*

*"¡Muy feliz año nuevo, Tío!"* Denise Sanchez said, opening the door wide to welcome him into her home—the setting of almost every family gathering and holiday celebration that Uncle Stanley had been part of since he'd moved to Bronco three years earlier.

"Bah, humbug."

His nephew's pretty wife smiled indulgently as she leaned in to kiss his weathered cheek. "I'd say that you're a week late expressing that sentiment, except that I heard plenty of the same at Christmas. And at Thanksgiving, too."

"I shouldn't have come," Stanley said, feeling a little guilty to know that his unhappiness would likely put a pall on the festivities. "I'm not really in a celebratory mood."

"I know." Denise hung his coat on a hook by the door, then hugged him tight. "But holidays are about *la familia* and we're not about to let you spend them alone."

And that was the true crux of the situation.

He *was* alone now, without the companionship of the woman he'd fallen in love with three years ago, the woman with whom he'd planned to exchange vows over five months ago.

He'd been so happy then. So full of hope for their future.

Until, on the day of their wedding, Winona disappeared without a word.

"Runaway bride," he'd heard one of the deputies say when they'd reported her missing.

That conclusion was followed by the snickers of his colleagues.

They'd tried to cover their laughter with fake coughs when

they'd realized that Stanley had overheard their remarks, but he wasn't fooled.

Nor did he believe for a minute that his Winona had run.

She'd been as excited about their impending nuptials as he'd been—thrilled to finally be a bride.

Sure, there'd been a few bumps in the road leading up to the big day, but they'd successfully navigated those together.

"I'm going to be a nonagenarian bride," she'd said with a laugh. "And since it's my first trip down the aisle, I might even wear white." She'd considered that possibility for only a brief moment before shaking her head. "Though probably not, because why would I forgo all the colors I love on the most important day of my life?"

It was a good point, he acknowledged. And while he'd always been a rule follower, his bride-to-be believed in making her own rules—it was only one of the many things he loved about her.

"People will talk no matter what I wear," she'd noted. "Because people have always talked about me. But I don't care. I've had my share of trials and tribulations, but I've also been blessed with an amazing daughter and granddaughter and grandchildren…and now with you." She'd looked at him then, her heart in her eyes. "I didn't think I'd ever fall in love again. And then you walked into my life and I couldn't imagine—didn't want to imagine—living even one of the rest of my days without you."

He'd felt exactly the same way, and their courtship had proceeded at a whirlwind pace.

If anyone had asked, he would have said that the years passed too fast to take things slow. But no one asked.

His family—his beautiful, wonderful family—had immediately loved Winona because he did.

His nephew and wife had always believed in sharing with others, and the first time he'd taken Winona to one of their wonderfully chaotic family dinners, neither Aaron nor Denise had blinked an eye. They'd embraced her person and her presence, simply shifting the place settings around to make room for one more and squeezing in another chair at the already crowded table.

He'd admittedly had some concerns about how they might respond to a new woman in his life. But they understood that he'd loved his wife with his whole heart for more than sixty years, and when Celia passed, he'd mourned deeply.

He hadn't been looking to fall in love again. In fact, he'd been certain that he never would. But he'd never imagined that he'd meet a woman like Winona Cobbs at Doug's bar.

*Love always finds a way.*

The echo of her voice in his mind made his heart ache.

She was right about that.

She was right about most things.

He knew there were some people who thought Winona was more than a little eccentric—and others who claimed she was cracked as a cracker—but he knew the truth. She was a gentle and generous spirit—though feisty when the occasion warranted—with a gift for seeing what others either couldn't or didn't want to see. In fact, they'd met at a "Free Psychic Reading" event at Doug's. And, only a few days later, they'd had their first official date at Pastabilities in Bronco Heights, where he'd fallen in love with her over fettucine and garlic bread.

Less than two months later, they were firmly established as a couple. And when he said grace before the Thanksgiving meal in this very house, he'd looked at all the familiar faces gathered around the table—his new love among them—and said a special thanks to the Lord for bringing Winona into his life.

This year, he'd railed at God for taking her away again.

Because how was Stanley supposed to go on without her?

The truth was, he couldn't imagine his life without Winona in it, and he was going to do whatever it took to find her.

# Chapter Six

"**Y**ou're late," Luca Sanchez said when his oldest brother settled on the vacant barstool beside him at Castillo's, a favorite local Mexican restaurant.

"And I'm not going to apologize for it," Julian told him.

"You were with a woman," Luca immediately guessed.

"Also not going to talk about it."

"Who?" his brother pressed.

Julian ignored the question, nodding to the bartender who wandered over. "*¡Hola!* Rafael."

"*¡Hola!*" The bartender returned the greeting. "What are you drinking tonight?"

"I'll have a pint of Modelo."

Rafael looked at Luca's nearly empty glass. "You ready for another?"

"Yeah," Luca replied. "Give us an order of *sopecitos* and some chile con queso, too."

"I already had dinner," Julian told him.

"Which won't stop you picking off my plate," his brother noted as Rafael set their drinks in front of them.

"What did you eat?" Luca asked when the bartender moved away again.

"Sweet-and-spicy chicken."

"Where'd you have that?"

"I made it."

His brother's gaze narrowed thoughtfully. "Which isn't a direct answer to my question."

"Well, it's the only answer you're getting," Julian told him.

"It's not like you to be so tight-lipped about a woman," Luca mused. "Or maybe I just don't remember because it's been so long since you've had a woman in your life."

"You're the only one who mentioned a woman."

"If you weren't with a woman, you would have told me where you were."

"Okay, I confess—I was with your girlfriend."

"Ha ha."

"That's right—you don't have a girlfriend," Julian noted.

"I'm too young—and far too popular with the ladies—to want to be tied down," Luca said immodestly.

"So why do you spend most of your free time here, hoping to catch a glimpse of Rafael's cousin?"

The bartender glanced over, a furrow etched between his brows. "You got your eye on one of my *primas*?" he challenged.

"No," Luca hastened to assure him, giving his brother a kick in the shins.

Rafael didn't look convinced. "It'll end up black if you start sniffing too close."

"I'm not eyeing or sniffing."

The bartender folded his beefy arms across his chest. "Why not? You don't think they're *bastante bonita*?"

"Are you comfortable there, between the rock and the hard place?" Julian asked his brother.

Luca glared at him.

"I'm sure they're *mucha hermosa*," he said, attempting to placate Rafael. "I'm just not looking for a relationship right now."

"The only thing he's hungry for are the *sopecitos*," Julian said, coming to his brother's rescue.

After a moment's hesitation, the bartender nodded. "I'll check on your order."

*"Dios, mano,"* Luca grumbled once Rafael had disappeared into the kitchen. "I'm not looking to tangle with a bartender who's also the bouncer in this place."

"Then you shouldn't be looking at Winter," Julian cautioned.

"I'm not looking at her. She's got a husband for that."

He snorted. "Her husband is good for nothing."

"Obviously she felt differently, or she wouldn't have married him." Luca nodded his thanks to Rafael for delivering their food. "But she should have ditched him at the altar, like *Tío* Stanley's fiancée did to him."

*Tío* Stanley was their great-uncle who'd moved to nearby Bronco a few years earlier, after the death of *Tia* Celia, his wife of sixty years. He'd adjusted remarkably well to the change in circumstances and had soon met and fallen in love with an older woman he'd planned to marry. Unfortunately his bride-to-be had gone AWOL before their wedding.

"Do you really think Winona just took off?" Julian asked, dipping a chip into queso.

"It's the only explanation that makes any sense."

"*Tío* Stanley doesn't believe it."

"He's hurting," Luca said, not unsympathetically, as he selected a *sopecito* from the plate. "But once he's had some time to think about it, he'll realize being single is better than being with the wrong woman."

Julian couldn't disagree with that, but he wondered how long he was supposed to wait for the right woman to realize that he was the right man for her.

When Ruby woke up the following morning, she had no expectations about when she might see Julian again. Sure, it was possible that their paths might cross in town one day, but considering that had only happened a few times in the last three years, she wasn't going to hold her breath.

And she certainly wasn't going to admit that she wanted to see him again. Because a single mom with two kids—an idea she was still getting used to!—keeping her busy every waking minute of the day had no business daydreaming about romance. Especially not with a man who was a friend of her ex-husband.

Even—or maybe especially—if being around him reminded her that she was a woman who'd ignored her own needs for far too long.

But when she responded to the knock on her door early the following afternoon, he was there.

This time, the bag in his hand bore the logo of the local hardware store. In his other hand was a toolbox.

"A new installation kit for your dishwasher," he said.

"Don't you have a ranch to run?" she asked, wishing that she'd taken an extra two minutes to put on some makeup that morning.

But between the baby and Emery, she'd felt lucky to steal ten minutes for a shower. And though she might wish she looked nicer, at least she was wearing clean clothes, aside from the little bit of baby spit on her sweater that dribbled past the edge of the burp cloth she'd put over her shoulder to avoid such mishaps.

"I'm hardly responsible for running it," Julian said. "I'm just a ranch hand."

"Still, my dad worked on a ranch, so I know very well that there are always things to do."

He shrugged, neither a denial nor an acknowledgment of her point. "It turned out that I had some time on my hands."

"And you want to spend it fixing my dishwasher?" she said dubiously.

"I figured you'd need it now that you have baby bottles to be sterilized."

Well, she could hardly deny that. "In that case, why don't you come in?"

As soon as he stepped over the threshold, Emery came running. "Hi, Mr. Julian."

"It's Uncle Julian," Ruby reminded her daughter.

"Did you bring doughnuts today, Unca Julian?" Emery asked.

"I didn't," he said apologetically. "Did you eat all the dough-nuts I brought yesterday?"

She shook her head. "But I like choc'ate ones best."

"I'll remember that for next time," he promised.

Emery nodded and headed back into the living room.

As Ruby preceded Julian into the kitchen, his words echoed in her head.

*Next time* certainly suggested that he anticipated stopping by again.

So maybe she hadn't imagined the crackle in the air between them the previous evening. Or the sparks that danced over her skin when he touched her the night before that. Or—

"Mommy, Jay's stinky again."

And just like that, Ruby was yanked back to reality.

"I guess we'd better take him upstairs to change him," she responded to Emery.

"Uh-uh," Emy said, scrunching up her face and pinching her nose. "You do it."

"Alright," she agreed, before turning to Julian to say, "I trust you don't need my help in here?"

"I think I can figure things out," he said.

She nodded.

"You stay out of Uncle Julian's way, okay?" she instructed her daughter.

"Okay," Emy agreed.

But when Ruby returned to the kitchen with a freshly bathed baby in her arms (because diaper blowout!), she found her dish-washer pulled out, Julian reclined on the floor with his upper torso somewhere inside her cupboard and Emery crouched be-side him, holding a flashlight.

She felt a quiver low in her belly as her gaze skimmed over the man—noting with appreciation the long, muscular legs clad in well-worn denim and flat, taut belly covered in soft flannel.

She'd grown up around cowboys, so there was no reason that she should suddenly be feeling weak-kneed around this one.

Or maybe she had secret handyman fantasies. After having been married to a man who didn't know how to change a light-bulb, perhaps it wasn't surprising that she'd find herself attracted to one who could not only identify a problem but knew how—and took the initiative—to fix it.

Whatever the reason for the sudden tingles in her veins, she was determined to ignore them.

"So much for staying out of Uncle Julian's way," she remarked dryly.

Emery immediately swiveled her head to look at her mom, a smile spreading across her face. "I'm helping Unca Julian."

"Helping or hindering?" Ruby wondered aloud.

"Helping," her daughter insisted.

"You are helping," Julian confirmed. "But you have to hold the light steady, remember?"

"I 'member," she said, turning her full attention back to the task at hand.

"I found the problem," Julian said, speaking to Ruby now. "You had a cracked drain hose."

"Can you fix it?" she asked.

"That's what I'm doing."

She settled Jay in his bouncy chair and moved to the sink to get a dishcloth to wipe Emery's breakfast crumbs from the table. But when she turned on the faucet to moisten the cloth, she got… nothing.

"Water's off," Julian told her.

"Oh. Of course." She felt foolish for not realizing that he'd have to cut the water supply to replace the hose.

She made do with the barely damp cloth, shook the crumbs into the sink. "I'm starting to realize that I've been letting my daughter coast," she said. "But now that I know she can help with meal prep and household repairs, that's going to change."

"Letting kids help is how they learn to do things. At least, that was the excuse my dad always gave when he put me to work as his apprentice."

"Is there anything I can do to help?" she asked.

"Nope." He slid out of the cupboard. "It's all done."

"Already?"

"I told you it was likely a quick job." He took the flashlight from Emery and turned it off. "Thanks for your help."

"You're welcome." She turned to her mom then. "Can I watch *Paw Patrol*?"

"If you watch TV now, you won't get any screen time later," Ruby reminded her.

Emery hesitated. "Can I read stories to Jay?"

"You can absolutely read stories to Jay," Ruby agreed. "And thank you for thinking of him."

Emery smiled as she skipped off to get some books.

Julian's brows lifted. "She can read? At four?"

"She won't actually read the books," she explained to him. "She does recognize some words, but she'll make up a story for him based on the pictures."

"Ah."

"I really can't thank you enough for the dishwasher repair," Ruby said.

"You could offer me a cup of coffee," he said.

"Do you want some day-old doughnuts with your java?" she asked.

"Why not?" he agreed.

She retrieved the carafe from her coffee maker and made her way to the sink. "Do I have water again?"

He nodded. "It will probably sputter a bit at first, but it will be fine after it runs for a minute."

She turned on the tap—and took a quick step back from the sink when the water did indeed sputter and spit coming out of the faucet. When it was flowing smoothly, she filled the carafe and set up the coffee maker.

Emery returned with a stack of books in her hands. She set them down on the table beside Jay's bouncy chair then climbed into her booster seat and picked up the book from the top of the pile. "This one is about a very hungry caterpillar," she said, showing him the cover. "The caterpillar eats lots of different things and turns into a butterfly."

"Spoiler alert," Julian said under his breath, making Ruby smile.

He smiled back.

"I'd almost forgotten that," he mused thoughtfully.

"That the caterpillar turns into a butterfly?"

"No," he said. "That your smile can light up a room."

An awkward silence grew between them, the only sound in the room coming from the drip of the coffee maker and Emery's storytelling.

Then Ruby glanced at the ceiling. "I don't think you're giving enough credit to the track lights over your head," she said lightly.

"I made you uncomfortable," Julian noted. "And that wasn't my intention."

"What was your intention?" she ventured to ask.

He shrugged. "I don't know that I'd consciously formed an intention—I just said what I was thinking." He hesitated another beat before adding, "Though I held back from adding how much I've missed seeing your smile over the past three years."

Her cheeks flushed—though her face wasn't the only part of her body that heated in response to his comment.

Desperate to defuse the tension that had suddenly arisen, Ruby glanced at Emery, preoccupied with her storytelling, and Jay, captivated by the sound of her voice. She cleared her throat. "It's sad, isn't it, how divorce affects so many other relationships?"

"It certainly can," he agreed.

"Coffee's ready," she said, when the machine stopped gurgling.

Julian reached into the cupboard for the mugs while she put the doughnuts on a plate.

She poured a splash of cream into her mug and stirred, at the same time wondering if putting more caffeine into her system was a good idea when just being near Julian already made her feel jittery inside.

She didn't understand what had changed between them.

She'd known him for years and always felt completely at ease in his presence.

But that was when he was Owen's friend and she was Owen's wife.

Now the status of both those relationships had changed, which meant that Owen was no longer between them.

Instead, there was an inexplicable tension that made her feel…not uncomfortable, she realized, but aware.

Aware of the fact that he was a very attractive man.

Aware of the fact that she was a woman who hadn't been with a man in a very long time.

And suddenly wondering what might happen if she breached the distance between them and touched her lips to his.

"Do you want to test it?" Julian asked.

Her startled gaze flew to his.

Because for just a second, she'd been certain that he was somehow privy to her inner thoughts and was suggesting that they test the chemistry sizzling between them.

Then she saw that he was pointing to the dishwasher with the half-eaten doughnut in his hand.

And she wasn't sure if she was relieved or disappointed.

"Should I run a test cycle?" she asked. "Are you not confident in the quality of your work?"

"I'm so confident, I'll offer you a warranty," he said.

"Let me guess, if I run the dishwasher and end up with water all over my kitchen, you'll give me back every dollar that I paid for the repair?"

"That sounds fair, don't you think?"

"I'll let you know."

He swallowed another bite of doughnut. "How long have you been washing dishes by hand?"

"Since Emery's birthday."

"That was almost four months ago."

She was surprised by his reply. "You remember her birthday?"

"Easy to do since it's three days before mine."

It was also exactly a month before Owen's, but Ruby wasn't sure her daughter's father would remember if his mom didn't remind him.

And she didn't want to discuss her ex-husband with Julian, so instead she said, "Well, thanks for the fix. Sincerely. I've set a strict household budget for myself to ensure I can put money in Emery's college fund every month, so I'm not sure how long it would have taken me to save up to call for a repair."

"My parents taught all their kids to be as self-sufficient as possible, so I'm pretty handy around the house," Julian said. "If you've ever got a leaky faucet that needs fixing or a light fixture that needs replacing, just give me a call."

"Or a Kelly doll stuck in the toilet?"

"I'm not sure that's something I've had to tackle before," he admitted. "Was it Emery's Kelly doll?"

She shook her head. "My sister's, way back when. But it was my brother who decided to let it swim in the toilet."

"Did your sister get her doll back?" he asked, amusement crinkling the corners of his warm brown eyes.

"My dad got out his drain snake and the doll was retrieved— and disposed of," she said. "Because Scarlett didn't want it back once she understood what else went down that drain. And my dad made Garnet buy her a new one with his allowance."

"I'll bet that was the last time he flushed one of her toys down the toilet."

"It was," she confirmed. "Though he came up with other creative ways to torment his sisters."

"As brothers are born to do," he agreed.

"Speaking of little boys," she said, as Jay started to fuss, "I think this one is almost ready for a bottle and an afternoon nap."

"And that's my cue to get out of your way."

"Oh. Okay." She refused to acknowledge the twinge of disappointment his words evoked. Of course, he wanted to make an escape—he had a life of his own and he'd already given her a substantial amount of his time over the past forty-eight hours. It was silly to feel disappointed that he was leaving when she hadn't even expected to see him today. "Well, thanks again."

Emery closed the book in her hands and shifted her attention to the adults in the room. "Unca Julian, will you play Candy Land with me?"

"Uncle Julian has to go now," Ruby told her daughter.

The little girl's bottom lip pushed forward.

"I don't *have* to go," Julian said. "I mean, it's not as if I've got anything on my schedule more tempting than Candy Land."

Emy's pout immediately turned into a smile. "I'll go get it!"

"You don't have to indulge her every whim, you know," Ruby said to Julian when her daughter had dashed off.

"Is it okay that I said I'd play with her?"

"Of course, it's okay. I just feel like we've monopolized your free time over the past couple of days."

"I can't think of anywhere else that I'd rather spend my free time," he said.

"In that case, you better be prepared for some fierce competition, because Emy won't hesitate to push you into the Chocolate Swamp if you get between her and the Candy Castle."

"Got it!" Emery said, returning to the kitchen with her board game.

Julian linked his hands together and turned them over to flex his fingers. "Game on."

* * *

"That spinner thing is rigged," Julian announced, when Ruby returned after settling Jay down for his nap. "Every time I got close to the finish, I landed on the peppermint candy and had to go back."

"How many times did she beat you?"

"I don't want to talk about it."

Ruby couldn't help but laugh at his petulant tone—and again when a grinning Emy held up her hand showing four fingers.

"Four times, huh?"

"I don't want to talk about it," he repeated.

"Do you want Mommy to play?" Ruby asked. "Give you some competition?"

Emy shook her head. "I wanna go 'bogganin' now."

"We can't go tobogganing just yet," Ruby said. "We have to wait until Jay wakes up from his nap."

"Is Jay gonna go 'bogganin', too?"

"I think he's going to have to wait a few more years before he tackles the hill."

"If Jay can't go down the hill, why do I hafta wait?"

"Because he won't be happy if we wake him up, and we can't leave him at home by himself."

"Maybe Unca Julian could stay?" Emery said, turning to look at him with a hopeful expression.

"You can't volunteer other people to do a job," Ruby admonished her daughter.

"I'm happy to help in any way that I can," Julian said.

"Except that I can't, in good conscience, leave my foster child in someone else's care."

"I understand," he said.

"It's not that I don't trust you," she hastened to assure him. "It's just that you haven't been vetted by Family Services."

"Have I been adequately vetted by you?"

"Unfortunately, that's not how it works."

"I was only going to suggest that I could take Emery to the park to go tobogganing," he said.

"Yay!" Emery clapped her hands.

"Your mom hasn't said *yes*," Julian cautioned the little girl.

"P'ease, Mommy!" The little girl wrapped herself around Ruby's legs and looked up, a pleading expression on her face.

"Let me think about this a minute," she said, tapping a finger against her chin as she pretended to contemplate. "If you're suggesting that I stay here with Jay, where it's warm and dry, while you go to the park to slide down snow-covered hills with Emery, then *yes*, I can agree to that plan."

"Yay!" Emery said again, racing to the hall closet to retrieve her coat and snow pants and boots.

"Do you have any idea what you're in for?" she asked Julian, when her daughter was out of earshot.

"I've been tobogganing before," he assured her.

"With a four-year-old?"

"Probably not since Marisa was four."

"Then I wish you luck."

After his third trek up the hill, dragging the sled with Emery on it, Julian was thinking that Ruby should have wished him energy instead of luck. He worked on a ranch, for goodness' sake. He was accustomed to physical labor. But apparently hauling a four-year-old kid on a sled was a different kind of physical labor. Or maybe it was that he'd volunteered for this assignment after working six hours at Blue Sky Beef earlier that day.

Whatever the reason, he was ready to drop when he finally managed to convince Emery that the hill was "all tobogganed out for today" and it was time to head back home. It helped that several other parents were rounding up their kids to leave the park, which suggested to Julian that it was probably close to dinnertime.

Of course, Emery wasn't his kid, but when he was with her

and Ruby, he couldn't help but wonder how his life might have turned out if he'd met Ruby first... For sure, he would have treated her a lot better than Owen McKinley did.

But that was all ancient history, and Julian was focused on the present.

"Look at you guys," Ruby said, when she met them at the front door. "All rosy cheeks and big smiles."

"Am I smiling?" Julian asked. "I can't feel my face."

"But you had a good time?"

"Yeah, it was pretty great," he said, and meant it.

"It was *the best*," Emery added.

"I'm a little surprised that you stayed out as long as you did," Ruby admitted. "Usually after four or five runs, she's worn out from the long walk back up to the top of the hill."

"Walk?" he echoed, his brows lifting.

Ruby looked at her daughter. "You didn't walk up the hill?"

Emery grinned. "Unca Julian pulled me on the sled."

Julian's gaze narrowed. "You told me that's what your mom does."

She responded with a cheeky grin.

"I did it *once*," Ruby acknowledged. "Then I decided that she could walk."

"I was conned," he realized. "Apparently by a master."

"It was fun," Emery said. "Thank you for taking me 'bogganin', Unca Julian."

"It was fun," he agreed, ruffling her hair. "And I would do it again."

She beamed at him.

"But next time, you're pulling *me* on the sled."

Emery giggled. "Uh-uh. You're too big."

"I guess we'll find out, won't we?" he said.

"It sounds like you burned off a lot of energy on the hill," Ruby remarked. "Are you hungry?"

*"Starving,"* Emery said.

"Go wash up for dinner then while I pop the garlic bread in the oven."

The little girl scurried off to do as she was told.

"I'll get out of your way and let you have dinner," Julian said.

"Oh, no, you don't," Ruby told him.

"No?" he asked, the question tinged with amusement.

"You fixed my dishwasher, and you pulled Emery up that hill countless times—I owe you dinner. It's not anything fancy," she said hurriedly, as he started to protest. "Just chili that I took out of the freezer this morning."

"And garlic bread," he noted.

"Which needs to go in the oven," she suddenly remembered.

After a moment's hesitation, he shed his coat and boots, then followed her into the kitchen. "Hot chili and garlic bread sounds like the perfect meal after several hours on the slopes."

"You were gone seventy-five minutes."

"Well, it felt like several hours."

She laughed softly. "I'm sure it did. So…you'll stay? Or did you have other plans for dinner?" she asked, realizing she didn't know what he did with his nights.

Julian held her gaze. "What kind of other plans do you think I might have?"

She shrugged. "A date, maybe."

"No," he said. "I don't have any other plans. And, Ruby?"

She'd turned to stir the chili in a pot on the stove, but looked back at him now.

"There's nowhere else I'd rather be."

# *Chapter Seven*

*Mustang Pass, Montana*

She couldn't sleep.

Winnie squinted at the glowing numbers of the clock on her bedside table.

2:17

She'd turned in hours earlier.

Long before midnight.

"I'm sorry," she'd said. "I don't think I can stay awake until the end of the movie."

The man in the La-Z-Boy recliner had shifted his attention from the television to her.

Not *the man*, she admonished herself. *Her husband*.

"Headache?" he'd asked.

She'd responded with a shake of her head. "Just tired."

"Okay," he'd said, as he paused the movie. "Get some rest. We'll save the ending for another time."

She'd kissed his cheek, grateful for his understanding, and made her way to her bedroom.

She *had* been tired, but sleep eluded her.

The same questions that ran on a seemingly endless loop through her mind all day continuing to plague her into the night.

So many questions.

Never any answers.

Beside the clock was a photo in a silver frame.

Though she couldn't see it in the dark, she knew it was there.

Her wedding photo.

Wasn't a wedding supposed to be the happiest day of a woman's life?

Why did she have no memory of that day?

No memory of her husband even?

"Post-traumatic brain injury," the doctor called it.

She'd responded to his diagnosis with questions:

"How long will it last?"

"When will I remember?"

Questions he'd been unable to answer with any certainty.

"It could be a few weeks. It could be several months. It might be that your memories of the past never come back."

At the time of his initial visit, it had already been weeks.

Since then, months had passed.

Still, she refused to consider that her past might be gone forever. There had to be something she could do to unlock the door to her memories.

Or pry it open, if necessary.

The man—*her husband*—had tried to help.

He'd taken her to all their favorite places around town in the hope that one of them might spark a memory.

The bank on Queen Street where they'd first met when he was a teller and she was making a deposit for Knit & Pearl, where she worked part-time.

Except that the bank was a pizza place now and the knitting shop had become a tattoo parlor.

"Signs of change," he'd noted with obvious regret.

But Winnie had no memories of what they'd been and so couldn't mourn their transformation.

Their next stop had been Riverside Park, where they'd apparently crossed paths a few weeks later and he'd picked a flower for her from the public garden and nearly been arrested for his efforts. A peony, he said. Pink and lush and fragrant.

She'd smiled at the story, though she had no memory of the meeting. But Victor claimed that she'd pressed the bloom in a book to preserve it as a memento, so it must have been a good day.

After the park, they'd gone for a bite to eat at the Main Street Grill—the diner where they'd gone on their first date.

It hadn't been anything fancy back then, either, he'd confided. Because he hadn't been able to afford fancy, but he'd wanted to ensure she got a good meal and there was a reason the diner had been an institution in Mustang Pass for more than fifty years.

She was grateful for his efforts, and it pleased her to hear the affection in his voice when he recounted events of their shared past. But visiting the gazebo where they'd shared their first kiss and the church steps upon which he'd proposed—also the church in which they'd exchanged their vows—triggered no memories for her.

Her mind remained blank, like a brand-new canvas awaiting an artist's brush.

Or like a newborn child who had yet to experience any of what life had to offer.

Except that she wasn't a baby—she was an old woman.

She didn't need to know her actual birthdate to know that— she just needed to look in the mirror. Her hair was white (though gloriously thick for a woman her age, if she did say so herself) and her face was deeply lined, like a road map of crisscrossing routes, proof of the miles that she'd traveled.

But why couldn't she remember any of them?

The loss of so many years wasn't just a source of frustration but sadness.

And while her husband was happy to fill in the blanks of the time they'd spent together, what about all the years that had come before?

She had absolutely no insight into those years.

It was almost as if she hadn't existed before she met Victor.

Was her husband the only family she had? The only friend?

*Where was Beatrix?*

She frowned at the question that popped into her mind seemingly out of nowhere—followed logically by another: *Who* was Beatrix?

Winnie felt a frisson of excitement, a tentative spark of hope.

Because even if she didn't remember *who* Beatrix was, she remembered her name. And now that she had, she instinctively knew that Beatrix was someone important to her.

A longtime friend?

A sister?

A daughter?

Her breath caught.

*Beatrix is my daughter.*

The burst of happiness was immediately smothered by darkness.

*"Don't take her away. Please. I need to see my daughter. My Beatrix."*

*"I'm sorry." But there was no remorse in the tone, no sympathy. "Your baby's dead."*

*"No!"*

*Strong hands gripped her arms, held her down.*

*A needle slid into her skin.*

A tear slid down Winnie's cheek as she finally drifted into slumber.

# *Chapter Eight*

*Tenacity, Montana*

Julian was surprised to get a text message from Hayes Parker early Friday morning, asking if he was available to meet. Intrigued by the request—and grateful for any kind of distraction that might keep his thoughts off Ruby for more than three minutes, Julian said that he was. Hayes replied with a time and a location.

But as he drove to the meeting location, his mind continued to drift back to Ruby—specifically the time he'd spent with her the night before. Conversation had flowed easily at the dinner table, and he'd been happy to stick around after the meal to occupy the baby while Ruby dealt with her daughter's usual bedtime routine. He'd been fighting his feelings for Ruby for a long time, but he had no weapon capable of combating his instinctive affection for her daughter. Maybe because he'd fallen for the little girl the first time he'd held her in his arms, when she was no more than a few weeks old. And he'd missed her, almost as much as he'd missed Ruby, when he'd ended his friendship with Owen.

The time he'd spent with them over the past couple of days had reminded him how much he'd enjoyed their company—and made him acknowledge that he was in danger of falling for the baby, too. But an even bigger problem was the feelings that had stirred inside him when he was alone with Ruby, after the kids were asleep.

If he thought that his feelings were one-sided, he might be able to ignore them, but the unexpected electricity that sparked whenever he and Ruby touched combined with some flirtatious banter and warm glances suggested otherwise. And if there was any chance that she might be attracted to him, he didn't want to ignore it.

Of course, figuring out what to do about it was a whole other issue. And one that would have to wait for further contemplation, because he'd arrived at the address Hayes had given him—which turned out to be directly next to the End of the Road Ranch, the property owned by Hayes's family.

Julian parked his truck on the road, behind the other man's vehicle.

"I'm guessing that you didn't have to travel too far for this meeting," he remarked, when he joined Hayes by the fence that ran parallel to the road.

"Not too far," Hayes agreed.

Julian tucked his chin into the collar of his coat and his hands into the pockets.

"I used to call it the End of My Rope Ranch," Hayes admitted. "When I left Tenacity, I never imagined coming back, never mind coming back to work as a rancher here."

"Ranching isn't for everyone," Julian noted.

"But for others, it's in the blood."

He nodded. "What is this place?"

"It's 800 acres that Henry Burkholder severed from his ranch and sold to Sam Gibson several years back. Sam planned to build a house on the land and start his own herd, but shortly after the papers were signed, his wife's grandfather invited them down to Texas to oversee his operation there."

"There are days that I'd choose Texas over Montana, too, if I had that choice."

"Winter days like this one, I'd guess," Hayes said.

"And you'd be right," Julian confirmed. "So why are we here?"

"Sam still owns the land. He wanted to make sure things worked out in Texas before he sold it—and then he forgot about it, or so he said when he contacted me to see if I might be interested in buying it and adding it to End of the Road."

"I assume you didn't call me out here to tell me that you're buying it."

"No," Hayes confirmed. "I called you out here because I thought *you* might be interested in buying it."

Hayes would know, because Julian had approached him a few months earlier, when he'd learned that End of the Road Ranch had fallen on hard times when Hayes's father, Lionel, was sick. But Hayes had rejected his offer to buy part of the land, determined to save every last acre—and perhaps prove himself to his always disapproving father.

A smile spread across his face as Julian nodded, overjoyed that his longtime dream might finally be within his grasp.

Ruby awoke Friday morning with mixed feelings.

Friday was usually the day that she looked forward to the weekend: two whole days to focus on Emery without giving a single thought to work. But this Friday came at the end of two weeks of holidays (aside from the New Year's Eve shift her boss had begged her to cover) and after the weekend, she and Emery would have to get back into their usual routines—and figure out how to fit Jay into them, too.

It hadn't taken any figuring—or even any effort—to find a place for the baby in her heart. From the first moment that Hazel Browning had thrust his car seat into her hands and he'd looked up at her with his big blue eyes, his expression far too solemn for someone so young, her mama bear instincts had kicked in. He was now one of her cubs, and she would do anything to protect him.

But how was she going to protect her own heart? Because she knew it would break into pieces when it was time to give him up.

And how was she going to protect her daughter's heart? Because Emery was growing more and more attached to the baby every minute of the day.

Thankfully, the little girl would be going back to preschool soon. Every day, she asked her mom how many more days before school started again. Ruby suspected she was more excited about seeing Mia, her best friend, than learning, but she figured the motivation wasn't as important as the desire to go to school.

Ruby had hoped to make arrangements for Emery and Mia to get together for a couple of playdates over the holidays, but the other girl's parents had taken her to Anaheim to visit her grandparents—and Disneyland.

Ruby's mom and dad had similarly tried to lure her to Florida with promises of visits to Disney World, but they didn't only want her to visit—they wanted her to move to the Sunshine State and had dropped more than a few hints about the abundance of job opportunities available to someone with her education and qualifications. And while Florida did boast over four thousand hotels compared to Montana's three hundred, Ruby couldn't imagine taking her daughter away from her paternal grandparents to placate the maternal ones.

Not to mention that Owen would likely have something to say about any decision to take their daughter out-of-state. And even if he didn't exercise his access on anything close to a consistent schedule, Ruby hadn't entirely given up hope that he might someday step up and be the kind of dad Emery deserved.

"Maybe Unca Julian will bring choc'ate doughnuts today," Emery said, drawing Ruby's attention back to the present.

"I don't know that we're going to see Uncle Julian at all today," she cautioned her daughter, reminded of the fact that he'd been a regular fixture in both of their lives before the divorce—and done a disappearing act afterward.

Thankfully, Emery had been too young to really remember him—or maybe, on some level, she did remember, and that's why she was already starting to get attached to him again.

"Why not?" Emy asked now.

"Because Uncle Julian has a job and other responsibilities. And it was nice of him to take time away from those things to hang out with us, but you shouldn't expect that he'll be a regular visitor."

Emery frowned at that, but before she could say anything else, Ruby's phone chimed with a text message.

She glanced at the screen and immediately chastised herself for the quick spurt of disappointment she felt when she saw it wasn't Julian's name on the display but her friend Lynda Slater's.

Apparently Emery wasn't the only one who'd hoped to see Julian again today.

An unexpected trial delay = time on my hands. Are you up for a visit?

She immediately replied:

Would LOVE a visit.

While she waited for her friend, Ruby found herself reflecting on their first meeting, three-and-a-half years earlier.

Emery hadn't been even six months old when Ruby started to hear rumors about her husband's infidelity. Though Owen denied having an affair, she knew that she had to take control of her future. So she made an appointment to meet with Megan Grant, the owner and manager of the Tenacity Inn, prepared to beg to get her old job back.

Thankfully, no begging had been required, and Ruby had been behind the desk the following Monday when a group of local lawyers arrived for a workshop. The subject was "Mediation vs. Litigation—Choosing the Right Path for Your Divorce."

Though she hadn't yet set her mind on ending her marriage, Ruby was intrigued by the title. And when there was a lull at the desk, she'd snuck into the back of the conference room in the hope that she might pick up some insights.

Apparently she hadn't been as unobtrusive as she'd hoped, because when the group adjourned for lunch, Lynda Slater—

the keynote speaker—came to the front desk and introduced herself to Ruby.

That impromptu conversation led to an unexpected friendship and they'd been besties ever since.

"Why doesn't anyone ever bring a veggie tray?" Ruby wondered aloud, as she took the dome-covered plate her friend offered.

"Because a veggie tray doesn't go nearly as well with coffee as cake does," Lynda replied, stepping into the foyer.

"Auntie Lynda!" Emy raced down the hall to throw herself at their visitor, wrapping her arms around her honorary aunt's legs.

Laughing, Lynda dropped her purse and the gift bag she still carried to lift the little girl into her arms.

"We got a baby," Emery told her. "A boy baby."

Lynda glanced at Ruby. "You finally got a call from Family Services?"

She nodded. "New Year's Eve. Or morning, I guess."

"Congratulations?" her friend said cautiously.

"It's a good thing," Ruby insisted.

Emy, bored with the conversation now, wriggled to be released. When Lynda set her down, she spotted the gift on the floor. "Is that a present?" she asked hopefully.

"It's a Christmas present," Lynda confirmed, in case the rosy-cheeked Santa on the bag wasn't an obvious giveaway. "Why don't you look at the tag and see who it's for?"

Emery peered at the tag tied to the handle, her eyes growing wide. "It has my name on it. It's a Christmas present for me?"

Lynda nodded. "Sorry I didn't get it to you before Christmas, but work was crazy busy right up until Christmas Eve and then, well, the holidays are always chaotic."

"Also, you don't have to bring something for her every time you come to visit," Ruby said to her friend.

"I don't bring something *every* time."

"Can I open it?" Emery asked.

"Of course you can open it," Lynda said, and Emery immediately started pulling tissue out of the bag.

"Take it into the living room," Ruby said. "I'll bring the cake and coffee in there."

By the time Ruby loaded up a tray with the coffee service, slices of cake and a juice box, Emery had the contents of the gift bag scattered on the living room carpet.

Jay, who had been fast asleep in the playpen when Ruby went into the kitchen, was now wide awake in her friend's arms.

"Look, Mommy. I got a coloring book and crayons and a new game and a Squishmallow and a LEGO set."

"Because Auntie Lynda doesn't spoil you at all," Ruby remarked dryly.

Her friend shrugged. "It's fun to shop for kids."

"Unless it's for formula and diapers."

"Good point."

"And you don't get your coffee until you give up the baby."

Lynda sighed but laid him down on the quilt Ruby had spread out on the floor.

Emery moved the box of LEGO closer to Jay and pointed to the 2+ age recommendation on the corner. "You can't play with this," she told him. "Cuz you're too little."

"I don't think you need to worry about him stealing your toys," Ruby assured her daughter. "He's not even crawling yet."

"I'm just telling him now so that he knows," Emery said.

"Well, he's probably going to need a reminder by the time he's mobile," Lynda told her.

The little girl wrinkled her nose. "What's mobile?"

"It means able to move around."

"When will he be mobile?"

Lynda looked at her friend, deferring to the expert on that question.

"Most babies start crawling when they're around eight months old and take their first steps around their first birthdays," Ruby said. "You took yours when you were eleven months old."

"Eleven?" Emery's brow furrowed. "Eleven's more than ten and I'm only four."

*Four going on fourteen*, Ruby thought.

"Eleven *months*, not eleven years," she clarified. "So it was about a month before your birthday that you started to walk."

"When's Jay's birthday?"

"November." Early November, according to the Family Services file, though the exact date of his birth was currently unknown.

"Is that a long way away?" Emery asked.

"It's January now," Ruby reminded her daughter. "Then comes February and March and…" She continued to recite the subsequent months of the calendar for her daughter.

"November's a long way away," she concluded, with a heavy sigh.

"After Halloween," Lynda said, to offer some additional context.

Em considered this for a long moment while she sorted her blocks into piles according to their color. "Maybe we can take him back and get a different baby," she finally said. "One that walks and talks."

Lynda choked on a mouthful of coffee.

Ruby slid her friend a look as she bit down, hard, on her own lip so she didn't laugh.

"Don't you think you'd be sad if Jay didn't live with us anymore?" she asked her daughter.

Emery nodded, apparently not needing so long to think about that question. "So maybe we can keep Jay and get another baby?"

"Or maybe we can be happy that we have Jay and take the best care of him that we can for as long as he gets to stay with us."

"Okay," Em agreed, picking up her new coloring book and crayons and carrying them to her child-size table on the other side of the sofa.

"So how was your New Year's Eve?" Ruby asked her friend now.

"A lot less eventful than yours," Lynda said, looking pointedly at the baby on the quilt.

"Didn't you have a date with…Brandon?" she prompted, remembering how excited Lynda had been when she told her about their plans.

"Brendan," her friend said. "And yes, I did."

"I'm guessing it didn't go quite as you'd hoped."

"Not quite," Lynda agreed. "He hit the bar early and got so drunk, he was passed out before midnight."

"I'm sorry."

Her friend shrugged. "So I hooked up with Callan."

Now it was Ruby who choked on her coffee. "Who's Callan?"

"Brendan's brother."

"O-kay," she said cautiously.

"Don't judge me," Lynda pleaded.

"I'm not judging you," Ruby promised. "I'm just… I'm not sure what I am, though envious is probably part of it because I haven't had sex since… I can't even tell you how long it's been."

Her friend frowned. "Please tell me that your worthless ex-husband isn't the last guy you slept with."

Ruby lifted her mug to her lips and swallowed another mouthful of coffee.

"You're not saying anything," Lynda noted. "Does that mean Owen *is* the last guy you slept with?"

"I don't know how to answer that question without telling you what you told me not to tell you," Ruby admitted.

"You've been divorced more than a year—and separated almost two years before that."

"I'm aware," she assured her friend.

"Are you telling me that you haven't had sex in *more than three years*?" Lynda's tone was incredulous.

Ruby nodded.

It was another fact of which she was well aware.

But truthfully, she hadn't given much thought to sex until very recently. In fact, not until she'd met up with Julian again.

"Well, I know what my resolution is for this new year," Lynda said. "To get you laid."

Ruby felt her cheeks grow hot. "I appreciate your interest in my personal life," she said dryly, "but getting naked with a man isn't on my 'to-do' list at the moment."

"Apparently it's been so long, you've forgotten how enjoyable sex can be," her friend noted. "Otherwise it would be at the top of your 'to-do' list."

"Maybe I have forgotten," she allowed. "But it's definitely not a priority right now."

"Sex—with the right man—should always be a priority."

"Well, having to be tested for STDs because my husband was cheating on me with multiple women should be proof enough that I don't have a lot of experience with the right kind of man."

"You won't hear any disagreement from me on that score," Lynda assured her. "But Owen was your past. It's time to move on from the past and enjoy your present."

Not wanting to discuss her current infatuation, Ruby retrieved the carafe from the kitchen to refill their mugs of coffee.

"Or maybe you already have moved on," her friend said in a considering tone.

"Of course, I've moved on," she confirmed. "My relationship with Owen McKinley is very much in the rearview mirror."

Lynda spooned more sugar into her mug. "Speaking of rearview mirrors—was that Julian Sanchez's truck parked in your driveway Wednesday afternoon?"

Ruby had to laugh. "That was a creative segue."

"Well, was it or wasn't it?" her friend prompted impatiently.

"It was," she confirmed.

"I didn't know you were…friends?"

"I'm not sure we are," Ruby admitted. "I always knew him as Owen's friend. But I guess we became friends, too, though we lost touch when Owen and I separated."

"So what was he doing here?" Lynda asked now.

"He brought juice boxes."

"Juice boxes?" her friend echoed dubiously.

"Apple and grape," Ruby said.

"I need more information than that," her friend insisted.

She sipped her coffee. "Julian was at the inn for the party on New Year's Eve when I got the call from Family Services, and he offered to come home with me to put the crib together so it would be ready for the baby when he arrived. Then he called the next day, to see how we were doing, and he heard Emery in the background, whining that we didn't have juice boxes, so he picked some up and brought them over."

"Well, isn't he a clever man?" her friend noted with a sly smile. "Currying favor with the child to score points with the mom."

"I think he was just being nice," Ruby said.

Lynda lifted a brow. "He just dropped off the juice boxes and then continued on his way?"

"Not exactly," she admitted.

"So why don't you tell me—*exactly*—what happened?" her friend suggested.

"He brought doughnuts as well as juice boxes, so I invited him to come in for a cup of coffee and a doughnut."

"And of course he said *yes*."

"He said *yes*," she confirmed. "And we had coffee and doughnuts."

"And then?" Lynda prompted.

"How do you know there's an 'and then'?" Ruby challenged. "Maybe that's the end of the story."

"It's not," her friend said confidently. "I know you—and the flush of color in your cheeks is a sure sign that you're flustered."

"Maybe because I feel like I'm being interrogated."

"Or maybe because a handsome, charming man is interested in you."

"Julian hasn't given any indication that he is interested in anything more than being friends." She sipped her coffee, then added, "Although he did stop by again on Thursday."

"With more juice boxes?"

"No. With a new drain hose for my dishwasher."

Lynda lifted her mug to her lips. "I cannot tell you how much I'm struggling not to say something totally inappropriate right now," she confided.

"I can see it on your face," Ruby said. "And I appreciate your restraint."

"Instead I'll just say that I'm glad you finally got the dishwasher fixed."

"Julian fixed it."

"Handsome *and* handy," her friend mused.

"And then Emery finagled him into taking her to the park to go tobogganing."

Her friend smirked. "Just being nice, huh?"

"You've tried saying 'no' to Emery," Ruby reminded her, rising from her seat to pick up the baby, who was starting to fuss.

"Okay, I'll give you that one," Lynda said. "And after tobogganing?"

"By the time they got back, it was dinnertime, so I invited him to stay and eat with us."

"It sounds like he spent the better part of two days with you."

"I guess he did."

"And after dinner?" her friend prompted.

"He said *thanks* and he left."

Lynda frowned. "Did he at least kiss you goodbye?"

"It wasn't a date."

"But did he kiss you goodbye?"

"No."

Her friend was visibly disappointed.

"But…" Ruby hesitated. "There was a moment. Or maybe a couple of moments."

"Tell me," Lynda urged.

And because Lynda was her closest friend in Tenacity and she desperately wanted to talk to someone about the unexpected stirrings she'd experienced when she was around Julian, she told her.

About the moment when his fingertips brushed against her palm when they were putting the crib together, and when their eyes locked in the foyer when she walked him to the door, and what he said about her smile lighting up the room.

"So there's something there," Lynda noted approvingly.

"Maybe," Ruby acknowledged. "But he was Owen's friend."

"And you were his wife," her friend retorted. "We all make mistakes."

"Touché."

"So when are you going to see him again? Tonight?"

"I don't know. He didn't say anything about tonight."

"And you're disappointed about that, aren't you? Because you want to see him tonight."

"I don't know what I want," she admitted. "But I do know this isn't a good time for me to be thinking about starting a romance."

"It's past time for you to move on," her friend said firmly.

"But I don't just have Emy to think about now—I've got Jay, too. And he's been through so much in his short life already."

Lynda looked pointedly at the baby now snoozing in Ruby's arms. "I think Jay's doing just fine. And God knows Emy could benefit from a father figure in her life."

"Mark spends a fair amount of time with her," she reminded her friend.

"And that's great. But he's her grandfather, not her father."

"Well, Julian isn't her father, either. And I wouldn't want her to start thinking about him as such and then have him disappear from her life…like Owen did."

"I don't think you need to worry about her getting too attached after one outing to the park."

"You're right," Ruby decided. "I'm being ridiculous."

"Or maybe you're worried that *you* might get too attached, because you already have feelings for him."

"I'm definitely attracted to him."

"A very good sign," Lynda assured her. "The question now is—what are you going to do about it?"

It was a question that Ruby continued to ponder long after her friend had gone.

# *Chapter Nine*

$A$s soon as Julian got home after his meeting with Hayes, he sat down at his computer and began crunching numbers, eager to put together an offer for the property.

"It's open," he called out, in response to the knock on his door.

*"¡Hola!"*

Recognizing his mother's voice, he closed the lid of his laptop and pushed away from the breakfast bar to greet her with a hug and kiss. "This is a pleasant surprise."

"I haven't seen you since the party at the inn on New Year's Eve," Nicole Sanchez said, the slightest note of accusation in her voice.

"I've been busy," he hedged.

"That's a surprise, as January tends to be a relatively slow month in ranching." Of course, she would know, as her husband worked in the same industry.

"And yet, there are always things to be done," Julian noted.

"Apparently," she agreed.

"Coffee?" he offered.

"A cup of decaf would be great."

He slid a pod into his single serve coffee maker and set a mug beneath the spout.

*"Gracias,"* she said, when he handed her the hot drink. "I stopped by yesterday afternoon with some leftover pozole, but you weren't home."

He brewed a second cup for himself. "I hope you left the soup."

She nodded. "It's in your freezer."

"Thank you."

His mom sipped her coffee. "Are you going to tell me where you were?"

"Visiting a friend."

"A *friend*," she echoed.

He immediately realized his mistake.

He was being evasive, and he was never evasive.

Not with his mom.

"A woman," she concluded.

"Yes, a woman," he admitted.

"Are you interested in this woman…romantically?"

"I am," he admitted. "But I'm not sure if my interest is reciprocated."

"Well, why wouldn't it be?" Nicole demanded.

Her indignant tone made him smile.

"I can only think that it's because she doesn't know me very well yet," he said dryly.

"When are you going to bring her home for Sunday dinner?" she asked, clearly unwilling to let the subject drop.

"I'll let you know."

"It's Sunday the day after tomorrow," she pointed out.

"So it is," he acknowledged.

"You'll be home for Sunday dinner?"

"When have I ever missed it?"

"Only when you've had plans with a woman."

"No plans this Sunday," he assured her.

"Well, there's always room for one more at the table, if that changes."

"It's very early days, *Má*. Too early to bring her home to meet the family."

"You let me know when you're ready and I'll make something special."

"Shouldn't you be busy making plans with Marisa for her wedding?"

"She doesn't want a big wedding or a big fuss—she just wants to marry the man she loves."

"And that's why you came here to fuss over me?"

"I can—and do—worry about all my children at the same time," she assured him. "Diego, Luca, Nina and Marisa as much as you."

"Your children are all grown up now, *Má*. Don't you think it's time for you to stop worrying and let us live our own lives?"

"I'll stop worrying when you've got a wife to take care of you," she retorted.

"I can take care of myself."

"Well, of course you can," she said. "I didn't raise my kids to be *tontos indefensos*. But a man alone isn't happy. You need a partner—*una esposa*—to share the good times and the bad."

"Thank you for the pozole, *Má*."

"You're welcome." She kissed his cheek. "Remember what else I taught you—to be respectful and careful. I want to be a *suegra* before an *abuela*."

Julian had managed to come up with an excuse to stop by Ruby's house every day since New Year's, but after assembling her crib, delivering juice boxes and fixing her dishwasher, he was running out of excuses.

So he was pleasantly surprised when, shortly after saying goodbye to his mother early Friday afternoon, his phone chimed with a text message from Ruby

Ran the dishwasher this morning… :)

His grumpy mood was immediately improved.

Because the brief—and admittedly impersonal—content of the message didn't matter as much as the fact that she'd initiated contact.

He pondered his reply for several minutes, because of course he was going to reply, and finally tapped out a message on his keypad.

The money-back guarantee is good for 60 days.

She answered quickly.

Since I didn't pay for the repair (and not even for the part!) I was hoping you'd let me make dinner as a 'thank you.'

Not such a brief or impersonal message this time, he mused.

And after a brief moment's hesitation, he tapped the telephone icon on the screen.

Ruby answered on the first ring.

"I'm not an efficient texter, so I thought I'd give you a quick call," he said.

"Apparently you have more to say than *yes* or *no*."

"I appreciate the offer…"

"But?"

"But you've got two kids to take care of—the last thing you need is to be cooking dinner for someone else."

"We all need to eat," she pointed out reasonably.

"Do you like pizza?"

"Doesn't everyone like pizza?"

"I assume that includes Emery?"

"It's only her second favorite meal in the whole wide world," she told him.

"So then is six o'clock okay for dinner?"

"Six is great, but I invited you," she reminded him. "So I should be the one to get the pizza."

"Next time," he said.


"Pizza!" Emery said, immediately identifying the flat box in Julian's hands. "Mommy, Unca Julian bringed pizza!"

"Well, I now know where I rank on her list of importance," he noted. "Below juice boxes, chocolate doughnuts and pizza."

"The way to a four-year-old's heart is through her stomach," Ruby told him.

"And the way to her mom's?" he asked, offering her a bottle of wine.

"I do like a nice chianti," she said, examining the label.

"Good, because the selection in the grocery store was limited, but a quick Google search promised that the simple flavors of a chianti would pair nicely with pizza."

"Well, I made a salad to pair with the pizza, too," she said.

"Because it's not okay to just have pizza?"

"The vegetables with dinner rule," she reminded him.

"Is that your way of guilting me into having salad, too, so that I'm not a bad example for your daughter?"

"You can eat whatever you want," she said, as she scooped some salad into Emery's bowl. "Your choices are between you and your mother."

She used salad dressing to make a smiley face on top of her daughter's salad and nudged the bowl closer to the little girl.

After Emy finished her salad, she ate two slices of cheese pizza. When she was done, Ruby excused her to go wash up and play.

Julian helped himself to another slice of pizza. "I seem to recall hearing that your family lives in Florida, which leads me to wonder how you ended up here."

"My parents are in Florida," she told him. "They moved down there about nine years ago. I actually grew up in Cody, Wyoming, where my dad worked on a cattle ranch until he was injured on the job and couldn't work anymore. After that, they took the insurance settlement he got and bought a little place in Madeira Beach.

"My brother, Garnet, is still in Wyoming. He works as a foreman on a different ranch there. And my sister, Scarlett, is a magazine editor in San Francisco."

"None of which tells me how you found your way to Tenacity," Julian pointed out.

"I went to Sheridan College in Wyoming to study hospitality

and tourism management. After graduation, I stayed in Sheridan for a few years, working as a desk clerk at a local boutique hotel. It was a decent job for a new graduate, though working the night shift was a bit of a challenge.

"I'd been there almost a year when I was contacted by one of those head-hunting agencies. They were looking for a suitable candidate to fill a vacancy at the Tenacity Inn. It was essentially the same job that I'd been doing in Sheridan, but days rather than nights and with the possibility of working my way up to a management position."

She shrugged. "And then I met Owen and got swept up into his vortex, which led to my career goals taking a back seat to his. And after Emery was born, I was happy to be a stay-at-home mom, to spend every minute with my baby. Owen approved of the arrangement, because it showed his colleagues that he was the breadwinner taking care of his family. But when he was at home with us, it was evident that he resented the time I spent caring for our daughter.

"He started spending more hours at the office and fewer at home. At least, he said he was at the office. And while I wanted to believe him, I'd heard rumors that he was hanging out at the Grizzly Bar a lot—especially when Debby was working."

Julian saw the emotion on her face and felt compelled to remind her, "Which only proves that he wasn't smart enough to appreciate what he had at home."

"You said something similar the other night," she noted cautiously. "But I thought you and he were good friends."

"We were back then," he agreed.

"Did he cheat on you, too?" she asked lightly.

"No, but he cheated on you, and I refused to pretend that his infidelity didn't bother me."

"So why didn't you tell me what he was doing?"

"There was a part of me that wanted to," he confided. "But

a bigger part knew that the truth would hurt you, and that was something I never wanted to do."

She nodded. "When we exchanged our vows, I really did believe it was 'till death do us part.' And, I'll admit, I considered staying with him for Emery's sake, because I thought it would be best for her to grow up in a home with a mom and a dad."

"What changed your mind?" he asked, as she settled back in her seat to give the baby his bottle.

"The realization that he wouldn't change—and that it was more important for me to be a good example to my daughter than stay in a marriage in which no one was happy."

"For what it's worth, I'd say you did the right thing. Emery is obviously thriving in the home you've created for her here."

"Thriving and impatient," Ruby noted, when her daughter interrupted them to announce that the numbers on the clock were an eight and a zero and a two.

"I know it's after eight o'clock, but I'm feeding the baby, so you'll have to give me a few minutes."

"But it's story time *now*." Instead of waiting, as her mom had suggested, she turned to Julian. "Will you read me a story, Unca Julian?"

He looked at Ruby for guidance.

She shrugged.

"Sure," he said.

The little girl beamed at him, and his heart swelled inside his chest. Oh, yeah, he was head over heels for this kid as much as her mother.

"You have to come up to my room," Emery said.

He rose from the chair. "What kind of books do you like? The *Twilight* series? *Harry Potter*? *War and Peace*?"

Her little brow furrowed. "I like *Max & Ruby*."

"Well then, I guess I'm going to have to learn about Max and Ruby."

"One story," Ruby said, calling out the reminder as Julian and Emery made their way upstairs.

"This is my room," Emery told him. "That's my bed and that's my dresser and that's my toy box and that's my bookcase and that's the chair where Mommy sits when she reads me stories." As she inventoried her furniture, she pointed to each item in turn.

Her room was decorated like a little girl's paradise, the walls painted a soft purple with ruffled white curtains on the windows and a chandelier dripping with sparkly glass crystals hanging over a bed that boasted a padded headboard in the shape of a crown and a hooked rug of Cinderella's carriage on the floor beside her bed.

No wonder the little girl ruled everyone in her world like a princess—she was born to the role.

"Is that where I'm supposed to sit?" he asked, gesturing to the glider rocker.

She nodded.

He took a seat while Emery perused the bookshelf. She picked one book, then a second and a third, then carefully carried them over to him. She set them on the small table beside the chair, then nimbly climbed into his lap.

"This one first," she said, reaching for the top book and offering it to him.

"Your mom said *one*," he reminded her.

She nodded. "*This* one."

He opened the cover and began reading *Max & Ruby's Snowy Day*, a story about a young bunny who wanted to play outside and his older sister's efforts to keep him occupied inside.

The story wasn't very long, and as soon as Julian had turned the last page, Emery reached for the next book on the pile.

"Now this one," she said.

Before he could protest, she tipped her head back to look at him with big blue eyes and said, "P'ease."

And there was no way he could refuse her.

And when he finished *Bunny Cakes*, he automatically reached for the last book.

He was nearly finished *Max's Bedtime* when he sensed Ruby standing in the doorway, her arms folded across her chest.

He flipped back several pages in the book to point to a photo where Ruby—the big sister bunny—was standing in an almost identical pose.

Emery looked from her mom to the picture and giggled, and Julian was certain it was the sweetest sound in the world.

"I said one story," Ruby reminded her daughter. "And now it's way past your bedtime, Emery Rose McKinley."

"Whoops!" Emery gave her mom a cheeky smile.

"Into bed with you," Ruby told her. "Now."

"Okay," the little girl said agreeably. But she gave Julian's cheek a smacking kiss before she slid off his lap, and his heart completely melted. "Thank you for reading to me."

"Anytime," he said, and meant it.

She smiled at him again, then hurried over to the bed, sliding beneath the covers her mom had pulled back.

"Night night, Em." Ruby bent down to give her daughter a hug and kiss. "Sweet dreams. I love you."

"Love you, too," the little girl said, her eyes already drifting shut.

"Am I in trouble?" Julian asked Ruby, as he followed her out of the room.

"I know it wasn't your fault," she said. "It's a little scary to see how easily she manipulates all the adults in her life."

"I did try to stick to the one-book rule," he said.

"Let me guess—she looked at you with her big blue eyes pleading as she handed you the second book."

"Apparently she does the same thing to you."

"She *tries* to do the same thing to me," Ruby said. "But mothers are made of tougher stuff than other mere mortals so that we can resist such obvious ploys. Most of the time, anyway."

He chuckled.

"But thank you for reading to her. I've been trying to keep her on her usual schedule as much as possible, but having a baby in the house has required us to make some adjustments."

"She's a great kid," he said. "I enjoy spending time with her."

"Is that why you've been here every day since New Year's Eve?"

"Well, I kind of like spending time with her mom, too. And I'm hoping, if she has a chance to get to know me better, she'll find that she likes me, too."

"Of course, I like you," Ruby said. "You're thoughtful and kind and patient and obviously great with kids."

"Maybe the word *like* doesn't paint an accurate picture," he allowed. "So I'll add the fact that I'm incredibly attracted to you."

She blinked. "You are?"

"I am," he confirmed.

"But…"

"But what?" he prompted, when she failed to complete her thought.

"But…you haven't even kissed me."

"No, I haven't," he agreed. "Because I've been waiting for some kind of hint that you might want me to kiss you."

Maybe it was the almost two glasses of chianti that she'd drunk, or maybe it was that being close to Julian made her feel a little wanton and reckless. Or maybe it was a combination of the wine and the man.

Whatever the reason, she stepped forward, breaching the distance between them, and said, "How's this for a hint?"

Then she touched her mouth to his.

It was supposed to be a casual, friendly kiss. A test of the chemistry that had been sizzling between them.

Instead, it turned out to be a spark that set off a firestorm of want inside her.

And maybe it had the same effect on Julian, because his arms came around her and he pulled her close, his tongue sliding between her lips, not just deepening the kiss, but fanning the flames already in danger of burning out of control.

She knew that playing with fire was a good way to get burned, but it felt so good to be in his arms.

To touch and be touched.

To want and be wanted.

But as much as she wished this moment would never end, she was achingly aware of the fact that she had a little girl not yet asleep upstairs who could wander down at any minute.

And so, with extreme reluctance, she finally eased her mouth away from his. But she stayed in the circle of his arms, her forehead tipped against his chest as she struggled to draw air into her lungs.

"That was…a pretty good hint," he said.

"A little more potent than I was anticipating," she admitted.

"And now I'm wishing we'd had this conversation on day one, then we might have enjoyed sharing kisses like that every day since then."

She laughed softly and looked at him, her expression serious. "I'm incredibly attracted to you, too, Julian."

"I'm glad to hear it," he said.

She should have taken a moment to think before she responded, but as if of its own volition, her mouth opened again and she heard herself say, "I might be lousy in bed."

The hint of a smile played at the corners of his mouth. "I don't think so," he said.

"But you don't know," she said. "After all, there must have been a reason that Owen preferred sleeping with other women to his own wife."

"Owen sleeping with other women was more about him than

you. For as long as I've known him, he's always had to be the center of attention. When you had Emery, he had to compete for your attention—or seek it elsewhere."

"That's an insightful observation."

He cupped her cheek with his hand, his thumb rubbing gently. "I'm sorry he hurt you."

She put her hand over his, savoring his touch. "I think I might finally be ready to move on."

"I'm glad to hear that."

They'd barely reestablished a friendship and their relationship was already changing again. And maybe it was too fast, but she was twenty-nine years old and she'd been alone for more than three years.

And Ruby didn't want to be alone anymore.

"Emery is going to her grandparents' house for a sleepover in a couple weeks," she told him.

"I'm sure that will be fun for her."

"It could be fun for us, too." She knew she was taking a step toward the point of no return and felt her cheeks flush as her body filled with tension.

Excitement.

Desire.

For Julian.

"If you wanted to have a sleepover here," she concluded.

His dark eyes immediately heated.

"It's a date," he promised. "Is there anything you want me to bring?"

She smiled. "A toothbrush."

# *Chapter Ten*

*Mustang Pass, Montana*

"What are you doing up, Winnie?"

She finished pouring the water into the pot before turning to face her husband. "I'm making tea."

"It's the middle of the night," Victor pointed out.

"I know, but I couldn't sleep." She reached into the cupboard for a mug, frowned at the row of cream-colored cups. Where was her favorite mug? The purple one decorated with the Mexican cherry flowers.

She gripped the counter as a sharp pain sliced through her head.

Victor was immediately at her side. "Are you okay?" He took her gently by the shoulders and steered her toward the table. "Sit down. I'll bring the tea to you when it's ready."

She sat and closed her eyes, and the pain in her skull receded a little further.

"Actually, it's not true that I couldn't sleep," she told him now. "I didn't have any problem falling asleep, but then I woke up."

"Bad dream?" he asked gently.

She shook her head, still mesmerized by the image of the brightly colored mug in her mind... "Strange dream."

"Do you want to tell me about it?"

"I dreamed about a man."

"Should I be jealous?" Victor was obviously teasing, and yet, Winnie had an uneasy feeling that the man in her dream was someone important to her.

"He was looking for something," she said, ignoring his question. "And he seemed...frantic. Or maybe desperate. Whatever it was that he'd lost was obviously important to him, and I wanted to help, but I couldn't get close enough to communicate with him. Every time I thought I was catching up to him, he'd go through a door, and when I went through the same door, I found myself in a big room, empty except for an old-fashioned writing desk."

"That is a weird dream," Victor agreed. "But you've always wanted to help other people."

"Have I?"

It was so frustrating that he seemed to know so much more about her than she knew about herself.

Nothing about this house or this town—or even her husband—was familiar to her.

"You have," he confirmed. "You are a warm, caring, loving woman, Winnie Thompson."

She could only take his word for it.

After she'd fallen and hit her head, she'd tried to do some research on traumatic brain injuries and amnesia, but it was hard to sort through all the information that was available online. And, truthfully, spending too much time looking at the screen made her head hurt.

So many things made her head hurt.

But her heart ached, too. Like there was a piece of it missing.

Victor carried her tea to the table and set it in front of her. "Have you had this dream before?"

"I don't think so." But even as she responded to his question, images flickered through her mind—like one of those old books with the pictures that seemed animated when you flipped through them quickly. The same room, the same desk, but different words written on the page.

*Don't believe them.*

*Help me.*

*Find me.*

*I want to go home.*

She lifted her mug to her lips and carefully sipped the hot tea.

"I just wish I knew what was real and what was fantasy," she said to Victor.

"You know I'm happy to answer any questions you have."

He was right—she did know. So why was she reluctant to ask the question that was at the forefront of her mind?

Finally she said, "Do we have a child?"

His face seemed to drain of color. He swallowed.

*Your baby's dead.*

The words echoed in her head again.

Had she and Victor lost a child? Was that why he seemed so shaken?

She reached out to touch his hand, feeling guilty for asking a question that obviously caused him pain.

He turned his hand over, to link his fingers with hers. "Don't you think, if you'd had a child, you'd remember her?"

"I don't remember you," she pointed out.

A flash of pain was reflected in his eyes, adding to the guilt already weighing heavily on her shoulders.

"I'm sorry."

"It's okay," he said, slowly withdrawing his hand from hers. "I understand that you're frustrated. I would be, too, if our situations were reversed."

She swallowed another mouthful of tea.

"Maybe we should talk to the doctor about giving you something to help you sleep," Victor suggested.

"I don't think a pill is the answer."

Maybe there weren't any answers.

Maybe it was time for her to accept that.

It was only when she was back in bed and staring at the ceiling in the dark that Victor's words echoed in her mind.

*Don't you think, if you'd had a child, you'd remember her?*

She'd asked about a child; he'd specified *her*.

Did he know more than he was telling her?

And if he was keeping secrets, were they to protect her? Or himself?

# *Chapter Eleven*

*Tenacity, Montana*

There was a time, Ruby mused, when visitors called or texted before stopping by.

Of course, it was possible that the woman standing at her front door Saturday afternoon was selling something or at the wrong address, because Ruby was certain she'd never seen her before.

"Can I help you?" she asked politely.

"Ruby McKinley?"

"Yes," she said cautiously.

"Danica Townsend." The woman held up the ID badge hanging on the lanyard around her neck. "Family Services."

"Oh," she said, admittedly taken aback. "Did I know that you were going to be stopping by?"

"No. This is what's called an unscheduled visit. I'm sure when the baby was left in your care, you were informed that a worker would follow up with both scheduled and unscheduled visits."

Ruby nodded. "Yes. Of course, I just didn't expect a visit so soon."

"I'd say that I had a break in my schedule," Danica said, "but the truth is, there are no breaks in my schedule so I squeeze in these visits whenever I can."

"Understandable."

"Can I come in?"

"Of course," Ruby said again, because she knew it was the only acceptable response.

The social worker unbuttoned her coat, which Ruby took from her. As Danica removed her boots, Ruby suspected that this unscheduled visit was not going to be a quick one.

"Mind if I take a look around?"

"Please," Ruby said, gesturing with her arms wide.

*My life is an open book.*

*Please let me keep the baby.*

*Maybe even forever.*

The last thought popped into her head without warning, making Ruby's heart jolt inside her chest.

She'd applied to be a foster parent to give a home to a child who needed one on an interim basis—she hadn't ever considered fostering as a stepping-stone to adoption. But now that Jay was here, she didn't want to imagine ever saying goodbye to the little guy.

Of course, she had to be prepared for exactly that eventuality. Without knowing the reasons that he'd been abandoned at the church in Bronco, she couldn't know that whoever had left him wouldn't come back for him at some point in the future—or that another family member wouldn't learn of his existence and want to give him a home.

Hers was only intended to be a temporary home for him, until his relatives—or a more permanent placement—was found.

Pushing that uneasy thought to the back of her mind, she refocused her attention on the social worker who'd started her self-guided tour in the living room. As Danica's gaze moved slowly around the space, Ruby tried to see it through her eyes—the blue faux-suede sofa and chairs with purple and turquoise throw cushions. The sharp edges of the coffee and end tables covered with clear silicone bumpers. The TV stand and bookcases anchored to the wall. Framed pictures of Emery—some posed and some candid shots—from birth to present, in silver frames on the wall.

The little girl's dedicated play corner was admittedly a bit untidy, but the colorful bins were filled with age-appropriate toys, puzzles and games. A playpen for Jay, empty except for a couple of soft fabric books and squishy blocks. Spread out on the floor in front of the playpen was the quilt made with different colors and patterns and textures that she used for tummy time with the baby.

The social worker checked some boxes on a page on her clipboard and scribbled some notes. Then she moved on to the kitchen.

"I've caught you in the midst of dinner preparations," she noted.

"Actually, dinner's ready to go in the oven," she said, sliding the pan of lasagna into the now preheated appliance. "You caught me before I had a chance to clean up."

Danica waved a hand, dismissing the smear of pasta sauce on the counter and the dishes in the sink. "You make your lasagna from scratch?"

"When I've got the time."

"I'm impressed."

She opened the refrigerator, surveyed the contents, added a couple more check marks to her page.

"Can I offer you anything to drink?" Ruby asked.

"I'm good, thanks." She eyed the high chair—empty. "Where is the baby?"

"He's sleeping. Upstairs." She gestured to the iPad on the counter, showing the video feed of the baby's crib.

"Is this his usual naptime?"

"One of," Ruby said. "He usually wakes around 7:00 a.m., then has a nap from ten thirty until noon and another between three and four thirty."

"Bedtime?"

"Between seven thirty and eight."

"Does he sleep through the night?"

"Not yet. He's usually up once around eleven thirty and then again at 3:00 a.m."

"Tough schedule for you," Danica noted.

"I can handle it," Ruby assured her. "It probably helps that I've been through it before, so I know this stage doesn't last forever."

"That's right, you've got a—" another glance at her file "—four-year-old daughter? Emery?"

She nodded.

"Is she in school?"

"Preschool. Half days, three days a week."

"Where is she now?"

"Building a snowman in the backyard."

"By herself?" Danica frowned as she made her way to the window.

"No." *As if.* "She's with a…friend of mine."

The social worker watched Emery and Julian for a few seconds before turning back to face her. "Boyfriend?"

"Male friend," she clarified.

"So you're not romantically involved with this friend?"

"No. I don't think so."

Danica's brows lifted. "You don't think so?"

Ruby felt her cheeks grow warm. "I'm trying to be honest with you," she said. "The truth is, I haven't dated since my divorce. Julian is a friend and we hang out together sometimes, but he did kiss me the other night."

"I didn't mean to put you on the spot or embarrass you."

"It's okay," Ruby said. "I know you need to have a complete picture of Jay's home environment and everyone in his life."

The social worker nodded. "So what is Julian's surname?"

"Sanchez."

"Any relation to Nina?"

"He's her brother."

"I went to high school with Nina."

"Small world," Ruby noted.

"Small town, anyway," Danica said with a smile.

Another glance at the iPad indicated that Jay was starting to awaken from his nap, so Ruby led the way upstairs.

The baby smiled when he saw Ruby—she hoped that earned her another check mark in the social worker's file—and snuggled into her when she lifted him out of his crib.

"He shares a room with you?"

"I thought it made sense to have him close—at least until he's sleeping through the night—so that he doesn't disturb Emery every time he wakes up." She set him on the makeshift change table to swap his wet diaper for a clean one, going through all the usual motions in the hope that the social worker wouldn't realize how unnerved she was by her presence. "When he's sleeping through the night, I'll move him into his own room across the hall."

Danica made some notes.

"Is it a problem that his crib is in my room?" Ruby asked, feeling a little anxious. "Ms. Browning didn't seem to think it was a problem."

"It's not a problem."

"He seems happy," Ruby said, refastening the snaps on his sleeper. Jay smiled at her again, doing his part to convince the social worker that he was content with the status quo. "I know he's only been here a few days, but he seems to have settled in."

"He does seem happy," the social worker agreed. "And, judging by the way he tracks the sound of your voice and responds to your touch, has already bonded with you."

"Well, that's good, isn't it?"

"It's good. And a little surprising, considering that he was with his previous foster mom for several weeks and has only been with you a few days."

She exhaled a cautious sigh of relief.

"I don't know if you want to look around up here some more," she said, "but this little guy is going to start fussing for his bottle."

"I think I've seen everything that I need to," Danica said, following Ruby down the stairs.

"Sounds like my snowman builders have come in from outside," Ruby noted, hearing voices in the laundry room, through which the backyard was accessed.

"Mommy! Mommy!" Emery charged through the door, her eyes sparkling with joy, her nose and cheeks rosy from the cold.

"We made a whole snowman family. A mommy and a daddy and a little girl snowman and a baby snowman."

She skidded to a halt when her gaze landed on the strange woman standing beside her mom.

"Who are you?" she immediately wanted to know.

"Manners, Emery," Ruby admonished.

"I'm Danica Townsend," the social worker told her.

"Can you say 'hello' to Ms. Townsend?" Ruby asked.

"Hello, Ms. Townsend," Emery said politely, albeit warily, understanding that her mom's words had been more a directive than a request.

"Ms. Townsend is a social worker with Family Services," Ruby explained, not just to her daughter but also for the benefit of Julian, who stood in the background looking every bit as wary as Emy. "She's here to make sure that we're taking good care of Jay."

"We are," the little girl was quick to chime in. "We feed him and burp him and change him. But only Mommy does the stinky ones."

The hint of a smile tugged at the corners of the social worker's mouth. "Are you happy that Jay lives with you?"

Emy nodded again. "It's like I have a brother now."

"What kind of things do you do with him?"

"*He* doesn't do *any*thing," the little girl confided. "But I read him stories and tell him about numbers and colors and hide behind my hands and then say peek-a-boo."

"Well, it sounds to me like Jay is a lucky little boy to have you."

Emy beamed proudly.

"And now I'll let you get back to your day," Danica said to Ruby.

She retrieved the woman's coat from the closet in the foyer. "It was nice to meet you."

"And all of you," the social worker said, accepting the proffered garment. Then she nodded to Julian. "Say 'hello' to Nina for me, Mr. Sanchez."

"Will do," he promised.

Ruby exhaled an audible sigh of relief when she closed the door at the visitor's back.

"Was it that bad?" he asked her.

"Actually, it wasn't bad at all," she realized, making her way to the kitchen to prepare Jay's bottle. "But I wasn't expecting a visit today, and then she was here, and I had a flashback to high school—to Mr. Zold announcing a pop quiz the one time that I didn't do my math homework."

"I would have bet you always did your homework," he said.

*"One time,"* she said again.

"Did you pass the quiz?"

"Barely. But Mr. Zold was concerned enough by my 'uncharacteristically low grade' that he made me take the paper home to get it signed by my parents."

"Ouch."

She nodded as she moved the bottle toward the baby's mouth. He immediately latched on to the nipple and started suckling. "The worst part is that my mother was 'disappointed.' As the big sister, I was supposed to be a good example to my siblings."

"I've heard that one, too," he assured her. "And I have two of each."

"Family dinners at your parents' house must be interesting with you, Diego, Luca, Nina and Marisa around the table. And Dawson now, too," she mused, adding his youngest sister's fiancé to the mix.

"You could come for Sunday dinner and experience it first-hand," he said.

She gauged that Jay had finished half his bottle and gently eased the nipple from his mouth so that she could burp him. "I don't think so."

"Why not?"

"Because…"

"*Because* isn't a reason," he chided.

"Because meeting the family is a big deal," she said, shifting the baby again to resume his feeding.

"You've already met my parents," he reminded her. "And you know Marisa."

"I met your parents the day I married another man."

"They won't hold that against you," he promised. "But since the idea of Sunday dinner with my family obviously makes you uneasy, we'll put it on the back burner for now."

"Thank you," she said. "And speaking of dinner, lasagna will be out of the oven in about twenty minutes, if you're interested."

"I think you know by now that I'm interested," he said, dipping his head to brush a light kiss over her lips.

"I was referring to dinner," she clarified.

He winked. "That, too."

Ruby worked 9:00 a.m. to 3:00 p.m. Monday through Friday, and occasionally picked up weekend shifts to pad her paycheck a little. Emery went to school on Tuesdays, Wednesdays and Thursdays, but only until 12:30, at which time her grandmother picked her up from school and then Ruby collected her from her grandparents' house when she finished work. On Mondays and Fridays, Emery went to daycare.

Except the Friday of her first week back at school following the holidays, when Caroline asked if she could take Emery to the new aquarium in Wonderstone Ridge. Apparently the facility was offering a special presentation for preschoolers, to introduce them to the various inhabitants of the oceans.

Ruby was grateful that Emery's paternal grandparents didn't only enjoy spending time with her but also made an effort to find activities that engaged her. As a result, Emery was always keen to go on "adventures"—as Caroline and Mark referred to their outings—with Mimi and Papa.

It was almost four o'clock Friday afternoon before they returned from Wonderstone Ridge.

"Did you want to come in for a cup of tea?" Ruby asked her former mother-in-law.

"That would be nice," Caroline agreed, ushering her granddaughter into the house.

"Did you have fun at the aquarium?" Ruby asked, as she helped Emery remove her coat and boots.

"So. Much. Fun," the little girl enthused.

"We always have a good time together," Caroline said, smiling affectionately at her granddaughter.

"I know you do," Ruby agreed. "And I'm grateful for all the time you spend with her."

"It's my pleasure."

Ruby knew she meant it. And it made her a little sad to think about everything that her own parents missed out on because they were so far away. But the move to Florida had been their choice, though one that had been made long before Emery was born.

Of course, Ruby made sure they got to FaceTime with their granddaughter every week, but a five-minute online chat was a poor substitute for in-person cuddles.

"What's that?" Ruby asked, when Caroline offered Emery the bag she'd carried in.

"Oh, just a couple of souvenirs that she picked out."

"You don't have to buy her something every time you go somewhere."

"I know," Caroline agreed. "But she really loved the dolphins, and they had an adorable stuffed dolphin in the gift shop. But then she couldn't decide between the dolphin and the orca. Then she saw the beluga whale and the sea turtle and the octopus."

As she inventoried the collection of toys that she'd purchased, Emery took them out of the bag and lined them up on the table.

"I appreciate your generosity," Ruby said sincerely. "But she already has so many stuffed animals on her bed there's barely room for her."

"It's hard to resist spoiling her a little," Caroline admitted. "Because she's my only grandchild—and likely the only one I'm ever going to have."

"Perhaps Emery can pick one to keep here and the rest can go to your house for her to play with when she's there?"

"That sounds like a fair compromise," Caroline said.

Emery apparently thought so, too, because she immediately picked up the dolphin and hugged it to her chest.

"Now put the rest of them in the bag so Mimi can take them home," Ruby instructed her daughter.

Emy dropped the octopus in the bag, then the beluga whale. Then she picked up the turtle and, after a moment's hesitation, tucked it into the crook of her arm with the dolphin.

"Emy."

She quickly added the orca to the bag.

"And the turtle," Ruby told her.

"This one's for Jay," Emy said.

"You know he can't have toys in his crib," Ruby reminded her.

"I know," her daughter confirmed. "But he can have it on the dresser, where he can see it."

"He can have it on the dresser," she relented, because how could she object to her daughter wanting to share her toys?

Emery skipped out of the room to take the turtle up to the baby's room.

"She is certainly fascinated with that baby, isn't she?" Caroline mused. "She hardly stopped talking about him all day."

"She is," Ruby agreed. "If a little disappointed that he doesn't yet walk and talk."

"It will happen soon enough." Caroline selected a couple of grapes from the fruit plate that Ruby had set out on the table. "She had a lot to say about Julian Sanchez, too."

The comment caught Ruby off guard, and she realized it

shouldn't have. Even if she hadn't been prepared for her four-year-old daughter to tell tales out of school, she should have been prepared for the fact that people might talk about his truck being parked in her driveway on several occasions over the past week.

"We happened to cross paths at the inn on New Year's Eve and rekindled our friendship."

"He and Owen used to be quite good friends."

"I'm aware."

"Of course you are," her former mother-in-law acknowledged. "He was the best man at your wedding."

"Would you disapprove of me having a relationship with Julian?" she asked cautiously. Because while she didn't think her personal life was any of the woman's business, she also didn't want to create any tension in their relationship.

"Would you stop seeing him if I said *yes*?"

She considered the question for a moment before shaking her head. "No."

Caroline nodded approvingly. "Good."

"Good?" she echoed, surprised.

"I hope that Mark and I will always be part of Emery's life—and yours—but you need to live your own life. To make plans for your own future and Emery's. And, because Owen and Julian were good friends for a long time, I can say, with some degree of authority, that he's a good man."

"He is a good man," Ruby agreed.

"You deserve a good man. You deserve to be happy. And it wouldn't hurt Emery to have another positive role model in her life.

"Don't get me wrong—Owen's my son and I love him with my whole heart," Caroline continued. "But I'm not completely blind to his faults. I know he wasn't a good husband. He didn't honor the vows you made and—even worse, in my opinion—he didn't respect you enough to end your marriage before breaking those vows. And he has a lot to learn about being a father.

"Which I really don't understand, because he had a wonderful example in his own father." She sighed now. "Mark and I wanted more children, but it wasn't meant to be. But when Owen married you, we got the daughter we'd always wanted, and the divorce didn't change that."

Ruby had to swallow the lump that rose in her throat before she could reply. "You and Mark have always been good to me and Emery."

"We'd be honored to be an interim Mimi and Papa to Jay, too."

"If he's still with us when he starts to talk, I have no doubt you will be."

"I don't think you need to worry about Family Services finding another placement for him," Caroline said. "Anyone can see that baby is exactly where he belongs."

Though obviously pleased by her former mother-in-law's observation, she was trying hard not to get her hopes up. Because Ruby knew that a reunion with his birth mother would probably be the best thing for the little guy, even if the possibility made her heart ache.

"The last I heard, they were still trying to track down his family," she said. "And the availability of family is an important factor in placement decisions."

"As it should be," Caroline agreed. "But family doesn't only mean those who are related by blood."

# *Chapter Twelve*

*Bronco, Montana*

Stanley was lonely.

More than five months after his planned wedding, he still hadn't heard a word from his missing bride.

His family had urged him to get over his heartache and move on, but he couldn't. And despite what everyone was telling him, he didn't believe for a minute that she'd run away.

If Winona had changed her mind about wanting to marry him, she would have told him so. She wouldn't have left him to wonder and worry.

And he was worried, because it was obvious that something untoward *had* happened. The blood on her porch proved it, even if his family had tried to keep that discovery from him, concerned that his broken heart would give up on him if he heard about it.

But his broken heart was somehow still beating, though his blood pressure went up every time he thought about how the police had bungled their investigation into Winona's disappearance. They'd been less than useless, insisting the blood wasn't proof of anything. And that was before Winona's daughter got a letter in the mail, purportedly from her mom. Because apparently a postmark from Portland, Oregon, trumped blood on a porch in Bronco, Montana.

Maybe he shouldn't blame the police, but he wished they'd shown a little more interest in the fact that his bride-to-be had told him, just a few days before their planned nuptials, that she'd seen a dark cloud in their future.

But even he'd brushed off her premonition as pre-wedding

jitters, and she'd acknowledged that was a possibility. Despite being ninety-seven years of age, she'd confessed that she was as nervous as a virgin bride at the prospect of becoming a wife for the first time. Probably because she was afraid of change.

For Stanley, the wedding was an even bigger deal. Maybe because he'd done it before and appreciated the significance of promising "till death do us part" in front of family and friends.

Was it death that had taken Winona from him, as it had already taken his beloved Celia?

No, he didn't believe death—or God—could be so cruel.

Like him, Winona had been in love before. But only once, when she was very young. She'd told him the whole story about her relationship with Josiah—the forbidden teenage love affair resulting in an unplanned pregnancy that caused her to be placed in a home for unwed mothers.

For years—decades!—Winona had believed that the baby she'd birthed had died almost immediately after. And she'd been so distraught by the loss of her child that the doctors had locked her up "for her own protection." Of course, when the truth came out—that her healthy baby girl had secretly been placed for adoption—she realized it had been for *their* protection. Because they'd known that she would have kicked and screamed until she found out what happened to her baby.

She'd been through so much in her life, endured so many ups and downs, experienced so many joys and sorrows. But she'd never been a bride. And while she'd originally pushed back against his efforts to set a date for their wedding, the closer they got to the day of the big event, the more excited she'd confessed to being.

So no, there was no way anyone was going to convince him that she'd simply changed her mind and walked away.

And, of course, he blamed himself for discounting Winona's concerns. Obviously, she'd been right to be worried.

But who would abduct a ninety-seven-year-old woman?

Why?

Stanley pondered that question as he measured coffee grounds into the filter and slid the basket into place.

He wasn't sure he even wanted coffee, but it was part of his routine, and going through the motions of his day-to-day routine was all he could do at this point.

But no matter what he did to occupy himself, he couldn't get Winona's disappearance out of his mind.

There had been no ransom demand.

Not that he had a lot, but he would gladly give everything that he had to get his fiancée back.

He was pouring coffee into a mug when someone knocked at the door. He started at the sound—and poured coffee all over the counter.

Cursing under his breath, he wiped it up and made his way to the door.

"Evan," he said, finding Winona's great-grandson standing there. "This is a surprise."

"Is it a bad time?" the other man asked.

"It's been nothing but bad times since my fiancée disappeared," he said. "But come on in."

Evan stepped over the threshold.

"How's your wife doing?" Stanley asked.

"Daphne's well. Eager to be done with being pregnant and get on with being a mom."

"And you?"

"Equal parts excited and terrified about being a dad."

"Kids are exciting and terrifying creatures," Stanley agreed.

Evan smiled at that.

"Can I pour you a cup of coffee? It's fresh."

"Coffee sounds great."

Stanley filled another mug and set it on the table. He gestured for Evan to sit, then took a seat opposite him.

"What's on your mind?" he prompted.

"I can't believe I'm going to tell you this," Evan said. "You know I don't believe in all that woo-woo stuff my great-grandmother is into."

Stanley nodded, because he did know—and that Evan had made Bronco Ghost Tours into a successful business despite not believing any of the otherworldly stories that he recounted for his guests. At least not until he'd met Daphne Taylor—now his wife—and the ghosts that lived at her Happy Hearts Animal Sanctuary.

"I feel silly even saying this out loud," Evan continued. "But...I think Winona is trying to send you a message."

He felt a frisson of excitement skitter down his spine. "And how exactly is she doing that?"

"Through my dreams."

"You've dreamed about your great-grandmother?"

"No. Well...not exactly."

"Well, what *exactly*?" he asked impatiently.

"For several weeks now, I've been having the same dream. About a locked room. The only thing inside the room is an old-fashioned writing desk, a feather quill and ink pot, and a piece of parchment upon which is written 'Don't believe them.'"

"'Don't believe them'?" Stanley echoed.

Evan nodded.

"Don't believe *who*?"

Now the other man shrugged.

"And you've had this dream several times?"

Winona's great-grandson nodded again. "The room and the desk are always the same, but sometimes the message on the paper is different. I've also seen 'Help me,' 'Find me' and 'I want to go home.'"

"You'd think, if she was sending a message, she'd be a little more direct about it," he grumbled.

"Knowing my great-grandmother, do you really think so?"

Stanley had to chuckle. "No, you're right. Winona always got a kick out of tangling people up with her cryptic messages."

He was surprised by the sound of his laugh—when had he last heard the sound? When had he felt so light?

But he had no doubt that Evan was right, that his dreams were evidence Winona was trying to communicate with him.

And while he might wish that she could have bypassed the middleman and come directly to him in his dreams, he understood that Evan—because he shared blood with his great-grandmother—might be more susceptible to receiving that sort of transcendental communication.

"Anyway, I don't know what it means," Evan said now. "And maybe it doesn't mean anything. But I thought you should know."

"You mean your wife insisted that you tell me?"

The young man's smile was wry. "That, too."

"Have you shared this information with the police?"

"No. And I'm not going to."

Stanley couldn't really blame him. The police had been skeptical enough about the blood; he suspected they'd put even less stock in dreams.

Which meant that he was going to have to figure this out himself.

And when he finally did, he was going to bring his bride home.

# *Chapter Thirteen*

*Tenacity, Montana*

On Monday, Julian took the pozole out of the freezer and heated it up for his dinner. As he savored the first mouthful, he decided that the hearty soup was good enough to forgive the intrusive questions his mother had asked on her previous visit.

He'd always been able to talk to her about anything, but he was admittedly a little bit worried that she might not approve of him dating his former friend's ex-wife. If what he and Ruby were doing could even be called dating, considering that all the time they'd spent together had been at her house.

Not that he was complaining.

He was just happy to be with her.

He enjoyed hanging out with Emery and Jay, too, but he couldn't deny that he was really looking forward to the night that Emery had a sleepover scheduled at her grandparents' house.

Of course, he knew Mark and Caroline McKinley well, having spent a fair amount of time at their house when he and Owen were in high school. They were good people and they'd always made him feel welcome in their home. He suspected they might look less fondly upon him now if they knew he was spending time with their former daughter-in-law.

He was just finishing up the dishes when a knock sounded on the door. Without waiting for an invitation, his sister Nina walked in.

"I need to start locking my door," he remarked, as she opened his refrigerator and helped herself to a can of Coke.

"I have a key," she pointed out.

"Remind me again why I gave that to you?"

She popped the tab on the can. "For emergencies."

"And is this an emergency?"

"Nope." She lifted the can to her lips and sipped.

"So what are you doing here, Nina?"

"*Má* sent me on a reconnaissance mission."

"Did she?"

"Of course, I'm not supposed to tell you it's a reconnaissance mission. I'm supposed to come up with a credible reason for dropping by and then work my way around to asking subtly probing questions about your new girlfriend."

"You wouldn't recognize subtle if it slapped you in the face."

"Which is why I didn't even try to go that route," she admitted.

"Am I supposed to applaud your forthrightness?"

"No applause necessary," she said. "Just give me something to take back to her."

He handed her the now clean and dry soup container.

"Ha ha."

"Tell her that it was delicious, as always."

"I need more than that, *mano*."

He pursed his lips, as if giving serious consideration to her request. "You could also mention that I finished the last of the tamales."

His sister muttered, creatively and colorfully, in Spanish.

"And that she should wash your mouth out with soap."

"She knows there's a new woman in your life," Nina said. "Someone that you're being uncharacteristically tight-lipped about."

"She's not a new woman."

"So…an old woman?" she quipped.

He rolled his eyes.

She narrowed her gaze. "An old friend?"

"Not any of *Má*'s business—and definitely none of yours."

"Which means she's someone we know," Nina realized.

"Why would you immediately jump to that conclusion?"

"Because if she wasn't, you'd tell me her name."

"No, I wouldn't," he denied. "Because you'd go home and cyberstalk her."

"I don't stalk," she said indignantly. "I creep."

"That's creepy, *mana*."

"*Creeping* just means following someone without their knowledge."

"Which is creepy," he said again.

"You can call it whatever you want," she told him. "But you know that I always find what I'm looking for."

Ruby wasn't expecting company when she was home with Jay on Tuesday—having booked a day off to accommodate his well-baby checkup, but recently Julian had been in the habit of stopping by, and the possibility that it might be him ringing the bell made her heart happy.

She should have peeked through the sidelight to confirm her suspicion, because it wasn't Julian.

Her smile slid from her face when she opened the door.

"Owen. What are you doing here?"

"I saw your car in the driveway and thought I'd stop in to see how you're doing."

It was credible that he was in the neighborhood; his office was only a few blocks away. But he'd never before stopped by without first communicating his intent—and even that was a rare event.

"I'm fine," she said shortly.

"You look good." His gaze skimmed over her, from the hair she'd pulled back into a ponytail to keep it out of the baby's reach, to the soft red sweater she wore over slim-fitting dark jeans. "Really good."

Once upon a time, it had taken nothing more than the look he was giving her now to make her knees quiver.

She felt nothing—which was sad but also a relief.

"Aren't you going to invite me in?" he prompted, when she failed to do so.

Ruby hesitated.

This was *her* house.

Her sanctuary.

Not that he'd never been inside, but he'd only been there half a dozen times before—and always to see their daughter.

"Emery's at preschool."

"I know."

But the slight hesitation before his response made her think that he didn't—that he hadn't thought about their daughter at all before he'd knocked on the door.

"I wanted to talk to you," he said.

Though she was still reluctant to let him in, she was even more reluctant to let all the heat inside her house escape through the open door. She finally stepped back.

She'd had no regrets about leaving the house where she'd lived as a bride and new mother. Divorcing Owen hadn't been an easy decision to make but it had been a necessary one, and she was grateful to be able to move on and make a fresh start with her daughter.

This house wasn't anything like the one she'd left behind, and it was filled with nothing but good memories.

It was hers and Emery's.

And baby Jay's, too.

*If only I could keep him.*

But she pushed those thoughts out of her mind as her ex-husband stepped over the threshold.

As he turned to close the door at his back, a muffled sound emanated from the baby monitor she'd left on the bookshelf in the living room.

Owen looked at her quizzically.

"I'll be right back," she said, ignoring the unspoken question in the lift of his brows.

She made her way up the stairs and into her bedroom, smiling when she saw Jay was on his side and peering through the slats of the crib.

"Look at you," she crooned softly. "You're going to be rolling over in no time—you're already halfway there."

He fell onto his back again as she approached and offered her a gummy smile.

"That wasn't a very long nap you had today," she noted. "Are you wet? Hungry?"

He responded with a gurgle.

"All of the above," she concluded.

She made quick work of his diaper change, reluctant to leave Owen unattended any longer than necessary. Not that she expected him to poke around—and not that she had anything to hide—she just wanted him gone.

When she returned to the main level with the baby in her arms, she discovered that her ex-husband had made himself at home—removing his boots and coat and helping himself to a cup of coffee from the pot on the counter.

He looked at the baby in her arms as he sipped his coffee.

"I didn't think that much time had passed since I last saw you," he remarked.

"Time really does fly, doesn't it?" she said lightly.

He frowned, as if not entirely sure she was joking.

"This is Jay," she said, setting the baby in his chair to free her hands to mix up his formula. "And he's hungry, so whatever you want to talk about, you can get started while I get his lunch."

"You're babysitting?" he asked, still stuck on the fact that she was caring for an infant.

"Fostering."

"Really?" he said, obviously surprised.

"Yes, really."

"Why?"

He was hardly the first person to ask her that question. Though he was the first to do so without any pretension of curiosity rather than disapproval.

"You know I wanted to have more kids."

It had been only one of many bones of contention during their short marriage.

"So this is how you're going about it?"

"Obviously this is a temporary arrangement," she said, more as a reminder to herself than an explanation to him. "But it's kind of fun to have a baby in the house again, and Emery is learning to be a big sister."

It was the perfect opportunity for him to follow up with a question about their daughter, to show an interest in Emy.

"I don't remember the early days being much fun," he said.

Dropping the ball, as usual.

*How would you know? You were never there.*

She managed to bite back the retort that sprang to her lips, because there was no point in rehashing old arguments.

Instead, she said, "Why are you here, Owen?"

"There's a rumor going around town that you've been spending time with Julian Sanchez," he finally said.

"Is there?"

His gaze narrowed. "Is it true?"

"My personal life isn't any of your business."

"I always suspected he had a crush on you."

"And I'm not interested in your speculations. But I am curious to know what makes you think you have any say about what I do in my personal life."

"You're my wife."

"*Ex*-wife."

"You're right," he acknowledged. "But the fact is, you were mine first—and that's the only reason he wants you now."

"My relationship with Julian has absolutely *nothing* to do with you."

"I can understand that you'd want to think so, but history would suggest otherwise."

"What are you talking about?"

"Ask your boyfriend about Laura Bell," he suggested.

Ruby shook her head. "No, I don't think I will," she said. "I'm not playing your games."

"Okay, I'll tell you," he said. "When we were in high school, Laura dumped Julian to go out with me, and ever since then, he's been looking for a way to get back at me."

"Julian doesn't strike me as the type of man to hold a grudge for—what?—seventeen years?"

"Maybe you don't know him as well as you think you do."

She eased the nipple from Jay's mouth and lifted him to her shoulder to burp him.

Owen watched her with the baby, an almost wistful expression on his face.

"I sometimes think I would have been a better dad if we'd had a son."

"Well, we had a daughter," she reminded him. "And you could be a better dad if you wanted to be."

"I just don't know what to do with her."

"What would you do with a son?"

He shrugged.

"Anything you think you might do with a son, you could do with your daughter," she pointed out. "Kick a soccer ball around, build Lego, go tobogganing."

"You think she'd like those things?"

"I *know* she likes those things."

He looked skeptical.

"The Winter Carnival is at the end of the month. You could start by taking her there."

"I've already got plans that weekend," he hedged.

"The whole weekend?"

"Yeah. I'm going to Big Sky to ski."

"She might like to learn to ski. I'm not suggesting that you take her to Big Sky," she hastened to assure him. "As I'm guessing your weekend plans include a woman."

He didn't try to hide his smile. "You know me well."

"But you could plan an afternoon outing someplace closer,"

she said, determined to get him back on track, to focus on what really mattered—before Emery was old enough to dismiss him as he'd dismissed her and the opportunity to know his child was lost to him forever.

"You don't think four is a little young to try skiing?" he said dubiously.

"She started skating lessons in October—you should see her on the ice now."

"My mom showed me a video," he admitted. "I was impressed."

She was lucky that Caroline and Mark took an interest in their granddaughter's life. She only wished Emery's father would show a fraction of the same.

"Speaking of Emery—it's almost time for me to pick her up from preschool."

"Oh." He glanced at his watch, frowned. "Doesn't my mom pick her up on Tuesdays?"

"When I have to work," she confirmed. "I took the day off because Jay had an appointment."

"Can you afford to be giving up shifts for a kid that isn't even yours?"

"Lucky for me, I get generous spousal support from my ex-husband," she said, tongue firmly in cheek.

"You didn't ask for spousal support," he reminded her.

It was true. When she discovered that he'd broken their vows, she'd wanted only two things—out of their marriage and custody of their daughter.

It was guilt, she guessed—or maybe pressure from his parents—that induced him to sign over title of the home they'd shared. And she knew he'd been annoyed that, as soon as the divorce was final, she'd sold that house to buy this one.

"Do you want to come with me—to say hi to Emery?" she asked him now. "I'm sure she'd be happy to see you."

He glanced at his watch. "Actually, I have to get to the office. I've got an appointment in fifteen minutes. But you can tell her that I said hi."

"Yeah, I'll do that," she said.

But it was a lie. She had no intention of mentioning his visit to her daughter, who'd already been disappointed by her dad too many times in her short life.

Between her job and caring for Emery and Jay, Ruby didn't have much time for anything else, but she was glad to spend that little bit of time with Julian, who stopped by almost every day. Sometimes his visits were brief; sometimes he stayed for a few hours. Ruby was always happy to see him and so focused on their blossoming relationship that, by the next night, she'd almost entirely forgotten about her ex-husband's impromptu visit.

Emery poked at the meat loaf on her plate.

"I don't like this."

"It's hamburger, Em."

Her daughter shook her head. "Hamburger has a bun."

"But it's the same kind of meat as a hamburger."

"I like hamburgers with ketchup."

Ruby got the ketchup and squirted a puddle of the condiment on her daughter's plate.

Though Emery still looked wary, she jabbed a piece of meat with her fork and dipped it in the ketchup. "Is Unca Julian coming tonight?"

"I don't know."

"He didn't come yesterday."

"He was probably busy."

Emery nibbled on the meat, made a face. "I don't like this hamburger."

"I'm sorry to hear that, because if you don't eat all your dinner, you can't have ice cream for dessert."

In short order, her daughter had cleaned her plate.

And maybe bribery wasn't recommended in any of the parenting books Ruby had read, but there were times when it was the only thing that worked.

As an added benefit, Emery's attention was so focused on her food that she dropped her questions about Julian.

But Ruby's worry lingered as she bathed Emy after dinner and dressed her in her pj's and helped her brush her teeth in preparation for bed. Because apparently her daughter had already developed an expectation of seeing him every day, and maybe she shouldn't have been surprised. Julian had been spending a lot of time with them and Emery was a little girl without a father figure, and obviously looking for a surrogate.

She'd always tried to do what was best for Emery, and she couldn't help thinking that the best thing might be for Ruby to stop seeing Julian before her daughter got too attached. The problem was she didn't want to stop seeing him.

Did that make her a bad mother? Or merely a selfish one?

But spending time with Julian had been good for Emery, too. Especially considering that, after Owen's most recent visit, Ruby didn't think he was going to step up to be a role model for his daughter anytime soon.

Or maybe she was just making excuses to justify her own relationship with Julian, because he made her happier than she'd been in a long time.

"Speak of the devil," she mused, when she peered through the sidelight (because that was a mistake she wouldn't make a second time!) and saw him standing on her porch.

Emery, having also heard the knock, had climbed on the sofa to look through the curtains. "It's Unca Julian, Mommy! He's here!"

She unlocked the door so that he could enter.

Before he could greet Ruby, Emery was there, jumping up and down to get his attention. "Hi, Unca Julian!"

"Hi," he said, lifting her into his arms for a hug. Then he met Ruby's gaze over the little girl's head, and his lips curved. "And hello to you, too."

It was crazy how his smile was enough to make her toes curl and her insides tingle, and to make her eager to know what other responses he might be able to elicit from her body.

"We didn't know if you were coming tonight," Emery said.

"I didn't know, either," he said. "I had some errands to run with my brother and I wasn't sure how long I was going to be." This time the look he gave Ruby was one of apology. "I should have called."

"It's fine," she said.

"It's late," Emery admonished. "You almost missed my story time."

"But *almost* means I didn't miss it, right?"

She nodded. "Are you gonna read to me?"

"If it's okay with your mom—" he glanced at her and got a nod of confirmation "—then I would love to read to you."

"Did you eat?" Ruby asked. "I could reheat some meat loaf for you."

"Thanks, but I grabbed a burger and fries with Luca."

"I had meat loaf and potatoes and carrots," Em told him. "*And* ice cream."

"What kind of ice cream?"

"Pink!"

"Strawberry?" he guessed.

She nodded.

"Can I tell you a secret?" Julian asked.

She nodded again.

He lowered his voice to a conspiratorial whisper. "Strawberry's my favorite."

"If you're hoping I'll offer you some, you're out of luck," Ruby said. "Em finished it off."

He pouted, doing a fair imitation of the little girl.

"But there's mint chocolate," Emery told him.

"Is there?"

"Uh-huh."

"Do you want some mint chocolate ice cream?" Ruby asked.

He shook his head. "I'm good, thanks. Besides—" he winked at Emery "—I don't want to be late for story time."

"Teeth need to be brushed before story time. Did you remember to brush your teeth after your bath?" Ruby asked her daughter, well aware that she had not.

"Whoops!" She immediately wriggled to be let down.

"Go do it now," she said, when her daughter's feet were on the ground. "And Julian will be up for story time in two minutes."

"That's how long the timer on my toothbrush is," Emery told him. "Don't be late."

"I won't be late," he promised. As soon as she was out of sight, he drew Ruby into his arms. "So I guess I have about a minute forty-five to say a proper *hello* to you?"

"Less than that, if you keep talking," she warned.

"Shutting up," he promised, and lowered his mouth to hers.

Julian enjoyed being part of Ruby's kids' bedtime routines. Even more, he enjoyed the long, lingering kisses he shared with her after Emery and Jay were settled down for the night. She was so passionate and responsive, and the soft sighs and quiet murmurs that emanated from her throat when he touched her drove him wild. But as much fun as it was to make out on her sofa as if they were teenagers, he was really looking forward to the opportunity—hopefully the following Friday night—to take their relationship to the next level.

First, though, tonight, there was something he needed to tell her. But it was hard to remember what that something was when she was on his lap, her knees straddling his hips, her lips cruising over his.

After several long minutes, she eased her mouth from his. "I'm really glad you decided to stop by tonight."

"Me, too," he said, sliding his hands beneath the hem of her sweater. "Because spending a little bit of time with you beats the hell out of no time at all."

She pouted. "Is that your way of saying you have to go?"

"Not just yet," he said. "There was something I wanted to talk to you about first."

"That sounds ominous."

"It's not," he promised, struggling to maintain his train of thought while she nibbled playfully on his lower lip. "I just thought you should know that Luca and I ran into Owen tonight."

She eased back now to look at him. "When you mentioned burgers and fries, I wondered if you'd gone to the Grizzly Bar," she admitted.

"That's it?" he said, surprised by her lack of reaction. "You're not interested in what he had to say?"

"Not the least bit," she promised.

"Because you heard it all when he stopped by to see you yesterday?" he guessed.

"And because he's my ex-husband," she reminded him. "Which means that I no longer have to care about his opinions on anything."

"So why didn't you tell me that he was here?"

She huffed out an exasperated breath. "Are we really going to waste the little bit of time we have talking about my ex-husband?"

It certainly wasn't his first choice, but now that he'd started down this path, he felt compelled to know where it ended. "I'm just curious to know why you didn't say anything to me about his visit."

"Because the only reason he stopped by was that he heard we've been spending time together and he wanted to stir up trouble, and I refused to give him the satisfaction."

Julian heard the annoyance in her tone, but he wasn't entirely sure if she was annoyed with him or with her ex.

Likely both, he acknowledged.

"What did he say to make you think he was stirring up trouble?" he asked her now.

"He told me to ask you about Laura Bell. And now my curiosity is piqued," she admitted.

"Are you asking me about Laura?"

"I guess I am."

"She and I dated through most of our junior year in high school—until she ditched me to go out with Owen."

"And now you're spending time with Owen's ex-wife," she noted.

"One thing doesn't have anything to do with the other," he assured her.

"Owen certainly thinks it does," Ruby countered.

"Well, he's wrong."

"So why are we even talking about this?" she wondered aloud.

"Because I know he isn't happy about the fact that we're together and I don't want him making trouble for you."

"He can't make trouble for me anymore," she assured him. "The only way he could hurt me would be to take Emery, and no judge is going to give custody to a man who sees his daughter—at most—three times in a calendar year."

"Okay," Julian said. "I just wanted to know that you were sure about us."

"I'm sure. And, anyway, whose happiness do you care about?" she challenged. "Owen's or mine?"

"Yours," he said, skimming his palms over the bare skin of her torso. "Only yours."

"Then maybe you could forget about my ex-husband and focus on me?" she suggested.

"I can do that," he promised.

And proceeded to prove it to her.

# Chapter Fourteen

As Will and Nicole Sanchez's kids grew up and got busy with their own lives, it became difficult to coordinate all their schedules and sit down for a meal together. The exception was Sunday night, when everyone gathered for a traditional family meal and the chance to catch up with what was going on in all of their lives.

On most nights, conversation flowed as freely as the sangria, but tonight, Julian was aware of pointed looks between his parents and awkward breaks in the conversation whenever a question was directed at him.

"Why do I feel as if this is some kind of intervention?" Julian asked warily.

"Is something going on in your life that makes you feel as if you need an intervention?" Luca asked.

"I could use some help with my interfering family," he said.

"Ha!"

"It's not an intervention," his mother said. "It's just Sunday night dinner." She passed him the roasted potatoes. "But I'd be lying if I said we weren't concerned about your relationship with Ruby McKinley."

He looked around the table. "Is that a collective *we*?"

"To be honest, I didn't even know you had a relationship with Ruby McKinley until right now," Diego said.

"Wait a minute," Nina chimed in. "This would be Owen's ex-wife?"

"Which is one of the reasons for our concern," Will remarked, turning his attention to his firstborn son. "You and Owen were friends for a long time."

"*Were* friends," he agreed, emphasizing the past tense. "We stopped hanging out when I learned he'd cheated on his wife and then walked out on his marriage and his daughter."

"And that's another reason," Nicole said.

"What's another reason?" he demanded, frustration seeping into his voice.

"Ruby has a little girl. And a foster child now, too."

"She has an adorable little girl," Julian noted. "And her foster child is pretty darn cute, too."

"Children are a complication, no matter how cute they are."

"And *Má* would know," Marisa chimed in. "Because she had five."

"I'm not saying it's not complicated," Julian allowed. "I'm just asking you to trust me to make my own choices."

"We do, *hijo*," his mother assured him.

"Apparently not."

"But we worry," she said.

"Don't you have enough to worry about with Marisa's wedding only a few weeks away?"

"As your brother pointed out, I have five children—I know how to multitask."

Julian didn't doubt it was true, but as adept as she might be, he knew there was no way she—or anyone else—would dissuade him from romancing Ruby.

"You seem a little distracted," Julian noted, as he helped his mom load the dishwasher after the interrogation masquerading as Sunday night dinner had ended.

"I'm worried about your great-uncle Stanley," she confided.

"Has something else happened?" Julian asked now.

"Denise called," she said, naming his dad's brother's wife who lived in Bronco and had daily contact with *Tío*. "Apparently Winona's great-grandson stopped by to see Stanley and got him all stirred up."

"Stirred up how?"

"He claimed to have some recurring dream that he believes is his great-grandmother's way of telling him that she's being held against her will."

"Do you believe it?" Julian asked her.

"It doesn't matter what I believe," she said. "What matters is that your great-uncle believes it. And now he's apparently made up his mind to go find her."

"It might be good for him to have a focus," Julian noted. "Since the wedding-that-never-happened, he's been…drifting."

"It would be good for him to forget about that woman and move on with his life," his mother said firmly.

"That woman was his fiancée," he reminded her.

"Who walked out on him the day of their wedding. And who does that to someone they claim to love?"

"I don't know," he said. "But I'm sure there's more to the story."

"Unfortunately, I don't think it's a story that's going to have a happy ending."

Ruby didn't realize how much of her daily routine revolved around her daughter until Emery wasn't there. Only an hour after Caroline had picked up her granddaughter for the planned sleepover, Ruby was showered, with dinner prepped and the dining room table set—complete with wineglasses, linen napkins and candles.

Without Emy flitting around the house, asking questions about this or wanting help with that, she was able to complete the requisite tasks in about half the time they would ordinarily have taken her. Not that she ever objected to her daughter's assistance, and if she hadn't been preoccupied by the fact that she was preparing for a DATE, she would have already been missing her daughter like crazy, though she had no doubt Emy was having the best time with Mimi and Papa and not missing her mom at all.

But she was preoccupied by the fact that she had a DATE and so she was relieved when Jay woke up from his nap and started fussing, because it gave her something else to focus on for a while. But after she'd changed him and supervised tummy time and read him some stories, he was content to sit in his bouncy chair and reach for the toys dangling above him while Ruby finished getting ready.

And now that was done, she had nothing to do but think about the fact that the evening was most likely going to end with her and Julian naked in bed.

Ruby hadn't been this nervous about a date since…

Since her first date with Owen, she realized with chagrin.

He'd been so handsome and charming in the beginning.

And the way he'd looked at her made her feel beautiful.

When had all that changed?

She couldn't say for certain, and really, the *when* didn't matter as much as the fact that it had changed. And the man who'd promised to love, honor and cherish her had broken every one of those promises.

Julian had made no such promises, and that was okay.

She knew that he was attracted to her, that he wanted to be with her, and for now, that was more than enough.

She fed Jay, then checked the potatoes roasting in the oven and stirred the chicken and vegetables in the pan on the stove. She sliced the crusty bread and set it in a basket on the table, then opened the wine—another bottle of chianti—so it would have time to breathe before dinner was served.

"What are the chances that you'll sleep until we're finished our dinner?" she asked the baby, as she carried him up to his crib.

He replied with a yawn.

"I'll take that as a good sign," she said, then gently touched her lips to his cheek. "Sweet dreams, baby."

He brought her flowers. A gorgeous arrangement of white roses, soft blue hydrangeas and deep blue delphiniums in a cobalt blue vase.

"I don't know much about flowers, but I thought they'd go well in your kitchen," he said.

"They will," she agreed, taking them there. "And they're beautiful. Thank you."

"Something smells amazing."

"Chicken cacciatore," she said. "And it's ready whenever you are."

"I could eat," he said. "But first…" He drew her into his arms and kissed her, long and slow and deep.

"I think I should cook for you more often," she mused, when he finally lifted his mouth from hers.

"That wasn't because you cooked for me. It's because I really like kissing you. And because I've been thinking about you— and about tonight—all day."

"Did you bring a toothbrush?"

"A toothbrush…and a box of condoms."

She was grateful he'd thought to come prepared, because that little but essential detail had slipped her mind.

Still, she couldn't resist teasing, "A whole box?"

"I don't expect we'll use them *all* tonight."

"But it's good to have goals," she told him.

He chuckled and kissed her again. "We could get started right now."

"Or we could have dinner first," she said.

"Whatever you want."

"Why don't you pour the wine while I dish up the food?"

They chatted easily over the meal, and by the time she was clearing their plates from the table, Ruby was feeling a lot more relaxed than she'd been a few hours earlier.

She was just about to take the lemon panna cotta out of the fridge when the baby started to cry.

"Looks like we're going to have to hold off on dessert until after I change and feed the baby."

"I don't mind at all," he assured her, rubbing his flat belly.

"Because I didn't know there was dessert when I agreed to that second helping of chicken."

"I shouldn't be too long," she said. "Why don't you see if there's a baseball game or something to watch on TV?"

His lips twitched as if he was fighting a smile.

"What's so funny?"

"You're not much of a sports fan, are you?"

"What gave me away?"

"It's January," he pointed out. "Not even the Grapefruit League plays in January."

"Hockey then?" she suggested as an alternative. "I know you need ice to play hockey, so I'm guessing it must be a winter sport."

"It is," he confirmed.

But he didn't turn on the TV.

As Ruby discovered when she returned to her now spotless kitchen and found him folding a tea towel over the oven door.

"Not a hockey fan?" she guessed.

"You did the cooking, so I did the cleaning—your rule," he reminded her.

"Well, thank you."

"You might not be so grateful tomorrow when you discover that I've put everything away in the wrong places, but you're welcome."

"Are you hungry for dessert now?" she asked.

"Yeah," he agreed, drawing her into his arms.

"I was referring to the panna cotta."

"I wasn't," he said, and lowered his head to kiss her again.

And her nerves were immediately dissolved by the heat that raced through her veins. Or maybe they hadn't completely dissolved, because he eased his lips from hers and tipped her chin up, forcing her to meet his gaze.

"Are you having second thoughts?" he asked gently.

"No," she said. "I'm a little nervous, but no second thoughts. Are *you* having second thoughts?"

"The only thought in my head right now is—how fast can I get her naked?" he admitted.

Ruby couldn't help but smile at that. "I just hope your… expectations…aren't too high."

"Is that your way of telling me that you don't have a stripper pole and a sex swing in your bedroom?" he asked teasingly.

"You've been in my bedroom," she reminded him. "Did you see either of those things there?"

"Maybe you put them in the closet when they're not in use," he suggested.

"You definitely need to lower your expectations," she warned.

"I don't think I do," he said. "Because all I really want is to be with you."

"It's been a long time for me," she cautioned.

"They say it's like riding a bike—as soon as you climb on, it will all come back to you."

She had to laugh at that. "Like riding a bike, huh?"

But as she took him by the hand and led him upstairs to her bedroom, she found the idea of climbing on wasn't a laughing matter but an arousing one.

Julian halted abruptly inside the doorway.

"What's wrong?" she asked.

"I forgot that there was a baby sleeping in your room," he admitted.

"The key word is *sleeping*."

He continued to hover by the door. "What if he wakes up?"

"I don't think he's going to have any idea what we're doing."

"Still… I'm not sure I'm comfortable getting naked with you in front of the baby."

Surprisingly, his apprehension made her less so.

She took a decorative throw off the arm of the chair in the corner and draped it over the slatted side of the crib facing her bed, so that even if Jay woke up, he wouldn't be able to see them.

"Is that better?" she asked.

"You're laughing at me, aren't you?"

"A little," she said. "But I also think it's sweet that you'd worry our...carnal activities might scar the baby."

"Carnal activities?" he echoed.

"Now you're laughing at me," she noted.

"A little," he said, drawing her into his arms.

He kissed her again then, long and slow and deep, until every last thought in her brain slipped away so that there was nothing but Julian. And still he continued to kiss her, making her feel not just wanted but cherished, and as he kissed her, his hands skimmed over her, touching her in a way that made her feel not just desired but adored.

She didn't realize he was unfastening the buttons that ran down the front of her blouse until she felt the air on her skin when the fabric parted.

He pushed the garment over her shoulders, let it fall to the floor. Then he unfastened her jeans and hooked his fingers in the belt loops to drag the denim over her hips and down her legs to pool at her feet.

He took a step back then, and his gaze was hot and intense as it skimmed over her.

"I really like your underwear."

"It's new," she told him.

His brows lifted. "For me?"

"For you," she confirmed.

"I appreciate the effort," he assured her. "But I think I'm going to like what's beneath the silk and lace even more."

He hooked his fingers in the straps of her bra and started to draw them down her arms, but she took a step back, shaking her head.

"No way am I getting all the way naked when you're still mostly dressed."

"I can catch up," he promised, already lifting his sweater over his head.

"Let me help."

She tugged his T-shirt out of his jeans and slid her hands beneath the hem. She explored the warm, taut skin of his stomach, tracing every ridge of his abdomen, the muscles quivering in response to her touch.

She hadn't thought about the fact that his work as a rancher would keep him in optimal physical shape, but she was thinking about—and appreciating—it now.

She touched her mouth to his chest, where his heart was beating as rapidly as her own. Then she tugged to release the button fastening his jeans and slid the zipper down. She dipped a hand inside, and he moaned as her fingers wrapped around him. He was hard—and huge—and that realization caused some of her hesitation to resurface.

It had been a long time, and she'd never been with a man as… built…as Julian. As she continued to stroke his velvety length, it occurred to her that inserting Tab A into Slot B might not always be as simple as it sounded.

He linked his fingers around her wrist, forcing her to halt her ministrations. "If you keep that up, *corazón*, I'm not going to be of any use to you."

Before she could respond, he lifted her into his arms, making the breath whoosh out of her lungs. It was such an unexpected and romantic gesture that she actually felt her heart flutter. Then he laid her gently on top of the mattress and lowered himself over her, straddling her hips with his knees.

"You are so beautiful."

It was hardly a unique line, but spoken in the husky timbre of Julian's voice and accompanied by the heat in his gaze, it didn't sound like a line at all.

"The way you look at me makes me feel beautiful," she confessed.

He brushed his thumbs over the tight buds of her nipples, through the silky lace of her bra. The brief contact made her gasp as arrows of pleasure streaked from the tips to her core. Julian hummed with satisfaction as his thumbs stroked the rigid peaks again, making her sigh. Then he lowered his head and suckled her through the fabric, first one breast, then the other.

Finally he located the clasp and released it, peeling back the lacy cups to reveal her bare flesh. Then his mouth was on her again, hot and wet, and his suckling was making her the same.

She was so distracted by what he was doing with his mouth that she didn't realize his hands were exploring farther south until he hooked his thumbs in the sides of her panties and drew them down her legs and tossed them aside.

"Julian." His name was a plea on her lips.

"Tell me what you want, *corazón*," he urged.

"I want you."

"I'm yours." He kissed her softly. *"Soy tuyo para siempre."* He slid a knee between her thighs, urging them apart.

She opened for him willingly, eager to feel his weight on top of her, his length inside her.

"Condom," she suddenly remembered.

He held up the square packet in his hand.

"Let me."

*"Un minuto,"* he said. "There's something I need to do first."

Then he lowered his head between her thighs.

"Julian," she said again.

He parted the soft folds at her center and put his mouth on her and her mind went completely, blissfully blank.

He tasted and teased with his lips and his tongue until everything inside her tensed and tightened and…finally… shattered.

She had to bite hard on her lip to hold back the cries of ecstasy that she wanted to shout out. He held her while she continued to shudder with the after-effects of her orgasm, and only when she stopped trembling did he speak.

"See?" he said. "Just like riding a bike."

The unexpected remark surprised a laugh out of her.

"I can assure you, if I'd ever experienced anything like *that* riding a bike, I would have spent a lot more time on my bike."

"Well, we're not done yet," he promised.

She took the square packet from his hand now and teased him with her touch as he'd teased her. When he was finally and fully sheathed with the condom, he again parted her thighs with his knees. But this time, when he settled between them, it was to bury himself deep inside her.

She wasn't prepared for the waves of pleasure to start again, but the sensation of him inside her was more than she could bear. And then he began to move, thrusting deep—and then deeper—and before she could catch her breath, she was freefalling again.

Julian was done.

No matter what happened between them going forward, he knew that there would never be another woman for him.

He'd been enamored with her from their very first meeting, but he'd had no choice but to get over his infatuation—or at least pretend that he'd done so. And while he'd dated plenty of other women in the past five years, he'd never felt about any of them the way he felt about Ruby.

He wanted to tell her that he loved her, because he knew that he did. But he also knew it was too soon—at least from her perspective.

By her own admission, she hadn't even dated since her divorce, so he didn't think she was prepared to hear such a declaration from the first man she'd slept with the first time she invited him to share her bed.

So instead of telling her, he showed her. With every brush of his lips and every pass of his hands, he showed her that she was desired and cherished. And when their bodies joined together, again and again in the night, he whispered what he knew in his heart.

*"Eres la única, mi corazón para siempre."*

*You are the only one, my heart forever.*

* * *

When Ruby awoke the next morning, in the warm comfort of Julian's arms, she was stunned to realize that it was almost seven o'clock.

"Good morning," he said, close to her ear.

"Good morning." She shifted so that she was facing him. "Did you sleep okay?"

"Very okay. How about you?"

"Better than I've slept in a long time. Apparently multiple orgasms are the key."

He smiled. "Happy to be of service."

She snuggled deeper into the warmth of his embrace. "It helped, too, that Jay slept through the night."

"Not quite," he said.

She tipped her head back to look at him. "What do you mean?"

"He was awake around four, fussing a little."

She frowned at that. "I didn't hear him."

"I'm glad."

"You changed him and fed him?"

"I've spent enough time here to know the routine."

"How is it that some lucky woman hasn't snapped you up long before now?" she wondered aloud.

"Maybe I was waiting for you."

She wanted to believe it could be true, that this amazing man really wanted to be with her, but she was wary.

Because she knew that she could easily fall in love with Julian, but she'd been in love before and look how that had turned out.

But even as the thought crossed her mind, she knew that she was being unfair to Julian. He wasn't anything like her ex-husband. And when it came to the day-to-day stuff, he'd already proven willing to show up and do the work that needed to be done.

Still, she was reluctant to rush into anything.

And she couldn't help but feel as if they were moving a little too fast.

Yes, she'd known him for years, but they'd shared their first kiss only two weeks earlier, and now she'd woken up with him in her bed.

And it wasn't that she regretted spending the night with him—how could she regret being with a man who had seriously rocked her world?—it was more that she had no idea where they were supposed to go from here.

Or even where she wanted to go.

"I forgot to ask if you had to be at the ranch early this morning, but I guess you don't."

"I texted the foreman last night and told him that I was going to be late today."

"How late can you be?" She slid her hands over his shoulders to link them behind his head. "I could fry up some bacon and scramble some eggs."

"As tempting as that sounds, there's something I'm even hungrier for right here."

So they made love again.

And a long while later, she sent him off with a lingering kiss and a travel mug filled with coffee.

"Can I see you tonight?" he asked at her door.

"Emery's going to be home."

"I'm not asking to spend the night," he said. "Just to spend some time with you—and Emery and Jay."

"We'll be here," she promised.

"Okay if I bring pizza?"

"You're angling to get my daughter to like you more than she likes me, aren't you?"

"If that was my goal, I'd bring pizza *and* strawberry ice cream."

And, of course, when he returned, it was with pizza and strawberry ice cream.

# Chapter Fifteen

"What should we do for dinner tonight?" Victor asked.

Winnie looked up from the book she was reading—or at least pretending to read, while her mind wandered far away from the words on the page.

"Dinner?" She glanced at the clock on the wall, surprised to realize that the day was more than half over already.

"Are you in the mood for anything in particular?" he prompted.

She slid her bookmark between the pages and closed the cover. "Since you asked, I've been craving tamales recently."

"Tamales?" he echoed. "Are those the Mexican things?"

"They're masa filled with meat and beans steamed in corn husks."

He made a face. "Doesn't sound appealing."

"What are you talking about? You love tamales. You must have eaten half a dozen last New Year's…" Her voice trailed off when she saw the worried look on his face. "Didn't you?"

"I don't think I've ever had tamales," he said. "Never mind eaten half a dozen of them."

"I could have sworn…" She frowned and rubbed at her temples. "Denise makes them with spicy pulled pork or slow-cooked chicken."

"Denise?" he immediately latched on to that name. "From the Main Street Grill?"

That's right, she suddenly remembered. Denise was the name of one of the servers at the local diner. The young one with the nice smile who wore her auburn hair in two braids.

So why was she suddenly certain that she was thinking about someone else named Denise?

Why could she picture a homey kitchen crowded with people and overflowing with laughter and love?

The memory—if it was a memory—made her heart swell with joy, if only for a moment.

"We don't know anyone else named Denise?" she asked.

Victor took her hand and gave it a reassuring squeeze. "I think maybe you've had one of your dreams again."

"Maybe," she said. "So many things are muddled up in my head."

"I know."

But she didn't want to spend any more time talking about the empty void where her memories should be. Instead, she asked, "What were your thoughts on dinner?"

"I was thinking that fish and chips sound good. We could go to the diner—maybe Denise will be working tonight."

"That sounds good," she agreed.

He smiled, obviously pleased by her response.

But it was a lie.

She didn't want fish and chips.

She wanted tamales, with a side of beans and rice.

Why was she lying to her husband?

Victor had never been anything but good to her.

Or at least for as far back as she could remember—which was admittedly only a few months.

Apparently when she'd tripped and fallen, she'd banged her head on the way down.

"You're lucky you didn't break anything," Dr. Hammond had said, when he'd come to the house to examine her.

But she didn't feel lucky.

Maybe her old bones were intact, but obviously something had broken in her mind and now everything in her past was hidden behind a dark curtain.

Like the heavy velvet curtains that separated the waiting area from the consultation chamber in a fortune teller's shop.

If only she could pull back those curtains and let in the light, illuminating the memories that were currently in the dark.

She closed her eyes, as if visualizing it might make it happen.

But instead of velvet curtains, she saw a purple door on a turquoise building decorated with stars and crescent moons. She instinctively knew the building was real—that it existed somewhere outside of her mind. And when she drew in a breath, she could almost smell sandalwood and vanilla.

She'd asked Victor about the possibility of seeing another doctor, but he told her that he'd consulted with three different specialists and they'd all said the same thing—that head injuries took time to heal.

"And even if you never remember what came before, we've got plenty of time to make new memories together," he'd said.

She wasn't entirely convinced it was true.

She was an old woman—whatever time she had left in this world couldn't be but a fraction of the years that had come before.

With a sigh, she opened her eyes first and then the cover of the book she still held in her hand.

But her mind continued to wander and her heart continued to ache.

So much time lost.

So many people forgotten.

*I'm sorry, Stanley.*

# Chapter Sixteen

*Tenacity, Montana*

Julian had grown up hearing the stories about his family history. His paternal grandparents had emigrated from Mexico shortly after they married, believing they could make a better life for themselves and their children in America.

Miguel had a knack with horses and quickly found work on a cattle ranch in Tenacity, Montana, and Liliana was hired to cook for the ranch hands. They eventually had two sons—Aaron and Will—and when the boys were old enough, they, too, were put to work on the ranch, learning everything they needed to know about ranching from their father and the other men they worked with.

Miguel's dream had been to earn enough money working on other ranches to eventually buy his own spread, then Liliana got sick, and a big chunk of his savings had gone to pay the medical bills. When the boys were old enough to follow their own paths, Aaron chose one that led him to Bronco, Montana, where he got a job with the post office and married a woman who worked in a hair salon. But Will only ever aspired to work the land as his father had done, and he remained in Tenacity doing just that, eventually marrying Nicole, another second-generation Mexican-American who helped support the family by tending their vegetable garden and working as a seamstress.

Julian was the oldest of their five children, and if at times it had felt cramped in their modest three-bedroom home, he'd been taught to appreciate what he had—a roof over his head, food on the table and family all around. And while money was often tight, there was always an abundance of love in their family home.

And Sunday dinner was an occasion not to be missed. Especially now that the kids were grown and living their own lives, it was an opportunity for them to reconnect and catch up.

Tonight they were dining on tacos al pastor.

"I have some news," Julian said, as bowls of meat and rice and various toppings were passed around the table.

"What news?" Will asked.

"I put an offer in on a parcel of land between the Barnhart property and the Parker ranch."

"To buy it?" Luca asked.

"No, to build a bridge on it," he retorted dryly.

His youngest brother rolled his eyes.

"And?" Nicole prompted.

He couldn't hold back the smile that spread across his face. "I got a call from the real estate agent on my way over here. My offer was accepted."

His mom's eyes filled with tears. "You're going to have your own ranch."

"You're going to be your own boss," his dad noted, nodding with satisfaction.

"That's the dream, isn't it?" he said lightly.

"Absolutely," Will agreed.

"You could be my boss, too, if you're hiring," Diego said.

Julian laughed. "I'm sure I'll be able to put you to work, but the final papers won't be signed until Tuesday and it's going to be a while after that before I get things up and running."

"But less if you had help," his middle brother pointed out.

"This is wonderful news," Nicole said, her eyes still misty. "Is there a house on the property?"

"Not a house," he said. "But there's an old hunting cabin. Just a couple of rooms in desperate need of repair—or perhaps demolition."

"Are you planning to live in that?" His mom sounded worried.

"No. As soon as the ground starts to thaw, I'll get started building a new house."

"Maybe by the time you do that, you will have met a nice girl to marry. Make sure you have lots of bedrooms for all the grandbabies you're going to give me."

He rolled his eyes, not yet ready to admit that he already had plans in that direction. "I'm not your only child," he reminded her. "Maybe one of your other kids can work on giving you grandbabies."

"I know, but you're the oldest."

"But Marisa will be the first to marry. In just a few weeks, in fact. So maybe you'll be an *abuela* in nine months…or less."

The bride-to-be, seated on the opposite side of the table, drew back her foot to kick his shin—but connected instead with Nina, seated beside him.

"Ow. What the hell, Marisa?"

Ordinarily her language would have drawn the ire of both parents, but Will was currently preoccupied looking daggers at his youngest daughter's fiancé.

"She's not pregnant," Dawson John hastened to assure his future father-in-law.

"I'm not pregnant," Marisa confirmed—this time finding her intended target with her kick.

"Of course, she's not pregnant," Nicole interjected, attempting to soothe her husband's wounded sensitivities.

"But I'm still hungry," Diego said.

Nina snorted. "There's a surprise."

And that quickly, the tension dissolved.

"Luca, pass the meat to your brother," Will said.

"Do we have more tortillas?" Marisa asked.

"Of course," her mom said, already pushing her chair away from the table to retrieve them from the oven.

As everyone refilled their plates and then their bellies, conversation ebbed and flowed around the table. Glasses were raised—and sometimes voices—as numerous and various topics were discussed.

To an outsider happening upon the scene, Julian imagined it might look like chaos.

To him, it was Sunday night dinner with *la familia*.

He loved each and every one of them, and he was looking forward to the day when Ruby, Emery and Jay had designated places around the table.

When Ruby decided to apply to be a foster parent, it hadn't crossed her mind that she might end up with an infant.

Of course, she'd been thrilled to get the call from Hazel Browning on New Year's Eve and would have happily opened her home to any child in need. But within the first twenty-four hours of Jay's arrival, she'd wondered how she'd ever managed to forget the work that was involved in caring for an infant.

Not that Emery was easy, but a preschooler was demanding in a different way. And when Emery was hungry or thirsty or tired, she told her.

Babies cried.

It didn't matter if they were hungry or wet or tired, they cried.

And it seemed as if Jay was *always* hungry or wet or tired.

But after only a few days, she started to distinguish his different cries.

It had taken a lot less time than that for her to fall head over heels in love with him.

And now, after almost three weeks together, they seemed to have settled into something of a routine.

When she was working, she put him in his playpen behind the counter, where he worked his charm on any and all of the guests who stopped by.

But nobody adored him as much as Emery.

Whenever Ruby picked her daughter up from Mimi and Papa's after work, the little girl greeted her mom with a big hug and immediately turned her attention to Jay.

Of course, most people couldn't resist a baby—especially one who had a smile for everyone he met. And that included Lynda, who came to the inn just before lunch on Tuesday with a paper bag bearing the logo of the local sandwich shop.

"This is a surprise," Ruby said.

"I brought meatball subs and pasta salad," her friend said, setting the bag on the counter so that her hands were free to steal Jay out of his playpen. "All I want in return are baby cuddles and details."

"What's the occasion?"

She stretched out her arms so that the baby was high in the air. His eyes went wide, then his mouth curved in a smile and he gurgled happily. "I kicked butt in court this morning and wanted to celebrate."

"You hate going to court," she said, well aware that her friend was a passionate advocate for mediation over litigation.

"But sometimes there are reasons the parties can't meet in the middle. In this case, the reason was my client's now ex-husband." She brought the baby close again, rubbed her nose against his, then lifted him high again.

"He just ate," Ruby cautioned.

"He wouldn't be the first one of your kids to throw up on me," Lynda noted, but she heeded her friend's warning and cuddled Jay close to her body. "Any update on the search for his parents?"

"Not that Family Services has shared with me."

"Want me to make some calls—see what I can find out?"

Ruby blinked. "You'd do that?"

"Anything for you, my friend."

It was an admittedly tempting offer, but she was afraid to push, afraid to risk changing the status quo. And absolutely terrified to think about what would happen if one of the baby's relatives came forward and offered to give him a home. "Thanks, but I think I'll pass for now."

"Okay," Lynda agreed. "Just let me know if you change your mind."

"I will," Ruby promised.

"Now I want to hear about the other man in your life," her friend said.

"Julian?"

Lynda arched a brow. "Do you have a romance going with someone else?"

"No."

"The last time we chatted, you were waiting for him to make a move," her friend reminded her. "Considering his truck was in your driveway after midnight Friday night, can I assume he finally did?"

"How do you know his truck was in my driveway Friday night?" Ruby wanted to know.

"Because I drove by on my way home from Callan's place."

"Callan? The New Year's Eve hookup that didn't mean anything?"

"A second hookup doesn't retroactively make the first any more meaningful," Lynda assured her. "And you are not going to distract me that easily."

"I wasn't trying to distract you. I was expressing an interest in your life."

"Back to Julian," her friend said, making it clear that the subject of her personal life was currently closed. "When did he finally make his move?"

"Actually, I made the move," Ruby confided.

"Well, well," Lynda said approvingly. "The girl's got game."

"I don't know if that's true," she protested. "But I did kiss him. And then I told him that Emery had a sleepover scheduled at her grandparents' house and asked if he might want to sleep over at mine."

"I want details of the sleepover. Everything but the sleeping part."

Ruby had to laugh. "All I'm going to say is that I can now happily assure you that the last person I had sex with was *not* my ex-husband."

"At least tell me that Julian's amazing in bed," her friend urged.

"He's amazing in bed," she dutifully intoned.

Lynda sighed. "I knew he would be."

"What do you mean—you knew he would be?"

"I guess this is where I have to confess that I had a crush on Julian in high school."

Ruby's jaw dropped. "And you're only telling me this *now*?"

Her friend shrugged. "I was afraid that if I said anything to you before, you'd be all weird about getting together with him."

"Well, of course, I would," she agreed. "There's a code."

"*I* had a crush," Lynda said again. "As in, my heart sighed every time he walked past me in the halls. He never knew I existed."

"I'm sure that's not true."

"Believe me, it's true," her friend insisted. "He was a junior and I was a freshman. And he was dating Laura Bell." She sighed wistfully. "Oh, how I envied Laura Bell. Until—"

"Until what?" Ruby prompted.

"Until they broke up," Lynda finished.

Ruby's gaze narrowed. "Until she dumped him to go out with Owen, you mean."

"I wasn't sure you knew about that," her friend admitted.

"Owen told me."

"Of course he did," Lynda said darkly. "Trying to make trouble for you and Julian, no doubt."

"It didn't work," Ruby assured her.

"Good. And I'm glad to know that my instincts about Julian were correct."

"Of course, I only have one night—and one morning—as the basis for my assessment, but he certainly exceeded all of my expectations."

"So why are you not doing it every chance you get?" her friend wanted to know.

"Because we're usually in the company—or at least the

proximity—of two children who, even when they're sleeping, could wake up at any moment," Ruby explained.

"You need to make time alone with him a priority. Make *him* a priority."

"It's a little scary, how quickly he's come to mean so much to me," she confided.

"Julian's not Owen," Lynda said gently.

"I know."

"And you deserve to be happy, Ruby."

"I am happy," she insisted. "I've got a good job, great friends and Emery and Jay. I feel like wanting anything more than that would be asking for too much."

"Trust me, wanting more orgasms is not selfish."

Ruby felt her cheeks flush. "You know that's not what I meant."

"I know," her friend admitted, with an unrepentant grin. "So tell me—do you have anything going on tonight?"

"No."

"Neither do I," Lynda said. "So reach out to Julian and set up a booty call."

She immediately shook her head. "I don't think so."

"You don't have to tell him it's a booty call. Just tell him that you've arranged a babysitter so that the two of you can have some time alone together. If he's half as smart as I think he is, he'll figure it out."

"You're really offering to babysit?"

"Why do you sound surprised?"

"Because it's not just Emery now," Ruby said.

"My sisters have six kids between them," Lynda reminded her friend. "Trust me—I've mixed more formula than a high school science class, changed a mountain of diapers and only once had to run to the emergency room because a kid got a Lego block stuck in his nose."

Ruby winced. "Thankfully Emy doesn't have any of the little blocks."

"It would require a concerted effort to shove a Duplo block into one of her nostrils," Lynda agreed. "But instead of thinking about that, go ahead and give Julian a call."

"Can I send a text message instead?"

"There are no hard and fast rules. You can do whatever you want."

She pulled out her phone and opened the messaging app.

"Sometime before seven o'clock tonight would be good," her friend remarked dryly, when Ruby continued to stare at the blank screen.

"I don't know what to say."

"Keep it simple. Something like—'Hey, Stud Muffin. Any plans for tonight?'"

She went with Lynda's suggestion, minus the 'Stud Muffin' part.

Any plans for tonight?

Julian glanced at the screen of his phone when it buzzed, surprised—and pleased—to see the text message from Ruby.

It seemed as if he was always the one reaching out, asking to get together. This was a welcome change.

He immediately replied:

Not yet. What did you have in mind?

He watched the three dots on his phone, waiting for her to finish composing her reply.

I have a babysitter. Maybe we could spend some time at your place?

His place? Was she suggesting a booty call?

Are you suggesting a booty call?

No!

The immediate—and undeniably indignant—reply made him grin, then the three dots appeared again.

Maybe...

And he laughed out loud.

Would you be interested if I was?

Do you really have to ask?

What time should I come over?

How long is your babysitter available?

Until ten(ish).

How about dinner first?

You don't always have to feed me.

I like feeding you. And I need to eat, too. Especially if I'm going to keep up my stamina for...after dinner.

He imagined her cheeks flushing with color as she read his response.

In that case, dinner sounds good.

Can I pick you up at 6?

I'll be ready.

# Chapter Seventeen

"You're not ready," Julian said, when Ruby came to the door with her hair in a ponytail, wearing a flannel shirt and leggings and a tired expression on her face. Not that he didn't think she looked great—because she did—but she didn't look like she had any intention of leaving the house.

She shook her head regretfully. "I'm sorry."

"Change of plans?" he guessed.

Now she nodded. "I tried calling you."

"I turned off my phone when I went into my meeting at the bank," he suddenly remembered, pulling the device out of his pocket now and discovering that he had three missed calls and a text message from Ruby. "Emery's sick?"

She nodded again. "Caroline called me after she picked Emy up from school to let me know she was complaining of a sore throat. So we stopped in to see the doctor on the way home and he did a rapid strep test, which was positive."

"Poor thing," he said, his personal disappointment immediately taking a back seat to concern for the little girl.

"She feels pretty miserable," Ruby agreed. "And is very unhappy that I'm making her keep her distance from Jay."

"Did the doctor prescribe antibiotics?"

She nodded. "I've got one dose into her so far. Anyway, I'm sorry about tonight."

"There's no reason to be sorry," he told her. "The only thing that matters is taking care of Em."

She blinked, as if surprised by his response. "Well, she's sleeping right now, so there's not much to do. But obviously I couldn't go out and leave her with a babysitter—not even her favorite honorary aunt."

"Obviously," he agreed. "And since we're not going to make our reservation at the restaurant, I'm going to call and cancel and then pop out to get us some food. Are you in the mood for anything in particular?"

She shook her head. "I'm not really hungry."

"Hungry or not, you need to eat—to keep up your strength so you can take care of your daughter."

"You're right," she acknowledged.

"How about a burger?" he suggested.

She considered for a few seconds, then nodded. "Actually, that sounds great."

"Do you need anything else?" he prompted. "Chicken soup for Em? Popsicles?"

"I've got soup. She might appreciate popsicles."

"What's her favorite flavor?"

"Banana."

He dipped his head to brush his lips over hers. "I'll be back in thirty minutes."

"I'll be here."

It took him a little longer than that, and the whole time that he was gone, he was anxious to get back to her, so that she wasn't alone.

It frustrated him to think how much she had to deal with on her own, as a single parent, because her ex-husband was less than useless. And though their relationship was still very new, he was eager to show her that she could count on him to be there for her and Emery and Jay, because he was as crazy about her kids as he was about Ruby.

When he returned, she was mixing formula and Jay was screaming in his high chair.

Julian put the popsicles in the freezer, set the bag of food on the table and unfastened the belt around the baby's middle to lift him into his arms.

The screaming immediately stopped.

"Thank God," Ruby said tiredly.

"I'm happy to help, but I don't think my assistance warrants deity status."

She managed a weary smile as she filled the baby's bottle.

"I'm sorry I was gone so long," he said. "It took me a while to track down Emery's banana popsicles."

"There's no need to apologize," she assured him.

When she reached for Jay, he instead took the bottle from her and nudged her toward the table. "Sit. Eat."

"I'll eat after I feed the baby."

"Do I have to call Chrissy to remind you that the correct response is, 'that would be helpful—thank you, Julian'?"

She lowered herself into a chair. "I don't mean to seem ungrateful."

"You don't seem ungrateful," he assured her, taking a seat across from her. "But you don't seem to know how to accept help when it's offered."

She didn't deny that it was true, choosing instead to focus on the contents of the bag. "Which one of these burgers is mine?"

"They're both the same." He settled the baby in the crook of his arm and offered him the bottle. Jay immediately latched on the nipple and began suckling.

"You got two orders of fries and onion rings," Ruby noted.

"I wasn't sure what you wanted—and I wanted both."

This time her smile came a little more easily.

"You mentioned earlier that you had an appointment today," Ruby remarked, as she unwrapped one of the burgers.

He nodded. "I planned to tell you about it over dinner, so that we could celebrate."

"What are we celebrating?"

He eased the empty bottle from Jay's mouth and lifted him to his shoulder to burp him. "I bought a ranch."

Ruby's eyes went wide. "What? You bought a ranch?"

"Well, I bought a parcel of land that's going to be a ranch," he clarified, returning the now satiated and sleeping baby to his high chair.

Her smile curved her lips and sparkled in her eyes. "That's exciting news."

"And a little bit scary," he admitted, unwrapping his burger. "Especially now that the papers have been signed."

"But this is your dream," she reminded him.

He nodded. "The first part of it, anyway."

She raised her paper cup. "Then I'm happy for you. And I have no doubt you will work hard to make it a success."

"It's definitely going to require a lot of hard work," he said.

"I wish we had something other than watered down soda to celebrate with."

"I'm just happy to be able to celebrate with you," he assured her.

"I really am sorry," she said again. "I know this isn't what you had planned for tonight."

"Please stop apologizing. And really, it *is* what I had planned for tonight—because I got to spend the night with you."

"Well, it wasn't what *I* had planned for tonight," she promised.

He reached across the table to link their hands together.

Inexplicably, her eyes filled with tears.

Julian immediately pushed away from the table to kneel in front of her. "What's wrong?"

She shook her head, but the tears spilled over. "I just didn't expect you to be so understanding."

"What did you expect?" he asked, baffled. "Did you think I'd be upset? Angry?"

She didn't say anything.

"Let me guess—Owen would have been mad?"

"He didn't like having his plans changed at the last minute," she admitted.

"Why are you still making excuses for him?" He wanted to know.

"I'm not." Her immediate denial was followed by a frown. "I am."

"Why?" he asked again.

She seemed to consider his question as she swallowed another mouthful of soda. "I think I do it for Emery," she finally said. "I always try to put the best possible spin on his actions so that she doesn't have to know that her dad's an asshole."

"I can understand that, though she's going to figure it out for herself soon enough."

"I know," she agreed. "And I hope you know how much tonight meant to me. Not just that you were so great about having our plans upended, but because you were here for me."

"You don't have to do everything for yourself, anymore," he told her. "You know that, right? You can call me if you need anything."

"I'm starting to believe that might be true."

"It *is* true," he assured her. "I'm here for you. Anytime."

"Thank you."

"I don't want your thanks. I want you to promise that you'll call."

"I'll call."

"Promise?"

She nodded. "I promise."

But she didn't need to call Julian, because he called her.

He texted the morning after their aborted date to check in on the little girl, then again later that day, and the following morning. Now it was Thursday afternoon, and he was on the phone again.

"How's Emery doing?"

"I'd say she's almost back to one hundred percent," Ruby told him. "In fact, she asked if she could go to preschool this morning."

"Did you let her?"

"No, I decided to keep her home another day to ensure she's fully recovered, though the way she's been bouncing off the walls should have convinced me." She was relieved that the antibiotics were working and her daughter was feeling so much better, grateful that her efforts to keep Emery and Jay apart had prevented him from getting sick, and wondering how she'd been lucky enough to have found a guy like Julian who seemed almost too good to be true. Someone who wasn't just a good man and a spectacular lover, but who made butterflies take wing in her stomach every time she saw his name on the display on her phone. Someone who made her want to trust and believe and take a chance on falling in love again.

"Good," Julian said, drawing her attention back to the present. "Because the Tenacity Winter Carnival is this weekend."

"We've never actually been to the carnival," Ruby admitted. "I considered taking her last year, but I wasn't sure if there would be much for a kid her age."

"There's something for kids of all ages. Snow sculpture contests, snowshoe races, sleigh rides, cocoa and cookies, and story time by the bonfire."

"It does sound like Emery might have fun," Ruby acknowledged. "But I'm not sure Jay would get much out of it."

"Nice try," he said.

"What do you mean?"

"You think I don't know that you're waiting for me to offer to take Emery so that you can stay home, cozy and warm, with the baby?"

She sighed wistfully. "Actually, that does sound like a better plan."

"Well, it's not going to happen," he assured her. "You're going to put on your thermal underwear and bundle up the baby and join us at the carnival."

"What if I'd rather wear the black satin underwear that was delivered today from Victoria's Secret?" She'd bought it on a whim, no doubt because Julian seemed to bring out the sexy side of her that had been hidden for so long.

"You do *not* play fair," he protested in a husky voice.

"I'm just curious to know what kind of underwear you'd prefer me to wear on the weekend."

"Wear the black satin under the thermal," he suggested. "The layers will help keep you warm and thinking of you in the black satin will keep *me* warm."

Julian was right—the Winter Carnival was fun.

And busy.

It was as if every single resident of Tenacity had come out for the event.

Emery loved every bit of it.

Ruby would have been happy to stay in the background, keeping Jay entertained—and warm!—while Emery dragged Julian from one activity to the next, but her daughter wasn't having it. Oh, she was happy to make snow sculptures with Julian, but she wanted her mom to be her partner for the snowshoe race. Then she dragged Julian around for the scavenger hunt and conscripted Ruby for the snowball relay. But the best, according to Emery, was the sleigh ride, because they all got to do that together—even Jay.

And though the air temperature was cold, it warmed Ruby's heart to see the joy on her daughter's face. When was the last time she'd seen Emery smile so widely? Or heard her laugh with such complete abandon? She honestly couldn't remember.

"Someone looks like she's having a good time."

Despite her earlier observation that all the locals seemed to have turned up at the event, it hadn't occurred to Ruby that her former in-laws might be there—or that, in the midst of the crowds, their paths would cross.

"I suspect this is going to become a yearly thing," Ruby said.

"It is for us," Mark said, smiling at his wife. "Every year since the carnival started."

"In the beginning, I don't know how they justified calling it a carnival," Caroline noted. "It didn't consist of much more than a snow-sculpting contest and a single booth selling hot cider back then."

"It's obviously a lot more than that now, because we've been here since noon and Emery has been going nonstop from one activity to the next."

"Kids do bounce back, don't they?" Caroline noted. "Looking at her now, you'd never know she was sick only a few days ago."

"They do," Ruby agreed.

"And how's this little guy holding up?" Mark asked, peering at the baby snuggled in the carrier attached to her chest.

"Surprisingly well," Ruby said. "I'm the one with frozen fingers and frostbit toes."

"You could head over to the bonfire to warm up."

"I'm hoping to head home to warm up, as soon as Emery gets her prize for completing the scavenger hunt."

"Mimi! Papa!" Emery, having spotted her grandparents, came racing over, waving her activity pack "prize."

Mark caught his granddaughter up in his arms. "How's Papa's princess?"

"I want snow taffy," she said.

"Well, who wouldn't?" he agreed.

"But wanting and getting are two different things," Ruby felt compelled to interject. "Because she's already had cotton candy, cookies and hot cocoa."

"That's a lot of treats in one day," Caroline remarked.

Emery tipped her head back against her grandfather's shoulder. "P'ease, Papa."

"I don't think your mom wants you to have snow taffy," he hedged.

"But do *you* want me to have snow taffy?"

Caroline pressed her lips together, obviously trying to hold back a smile.

"That child is going to rule the world someday," Julian remarked.

Mark lifted a brow. "Someday?"

"You didn't answer my question, Papa," Emery said.

"I want your mom to not be mad at me," he finally said. "So that means no snow taffy today."

"Tomorrow?"

He had to chuckle. "Let's wait and see what tomorrow brings."

"And right now, we need to be heading home," Ruby said. "So give Mimi and Papa hugs and kisses."

The little girl dutifully spread the love, and when Mark set her on her feet again, she returned to Julian's side to put her mittened hand in his.

"It was good to see you again, Julian," Mark said.

"And both of you," he replied.

As the McKinleys wandered off—in the direction of the snow taffy booth—Ruby and Julian turned toward home with the kids.

"Was that awkward?" Ruby asked cautiously.

"A lot less than I expected," he said.

"Me, too," she agreed. "But they're important to Emy—and me—so I'm glad that they seem to be okay with you and me dating."

For several seconds, the only sound was the crunch of their boots in the snow, then Julian asked, "Is that what we're doing—dating?"

Ruby wasn't entirely sure how to interpret his question—or his guarded tone. "Isn't it?"

Before he could respond, Emery abruptly halted in the middle of the sidewalk and tipped her head back to look up at Julian. "My legs are s'eepy."

"Do you want me to carry you?" he offered.

The little girl nodded, making the red pompom on her hat bounce. "Yes, p'ease."

Julian lifted her into his arms and carried her the rest of the way home, and Ruby breathed a quiet sigh of relief that the discussion of their relationship was effectively shelved—at least for the moment.

But later that night, after the kids had been fed and bathed and were tucked into their respective beds, and she and Julian were settled on the sofa with glasses of wine, he picked up the conversation right where they'd left off.

"So, dating, huh?"

"You don't want to date me?" she asked, attempting to keep her tone—and the conversation—light.

"I was actually hoping that our relationship might have a slightly higher status," he said, unwilling to follow her cue.

Ruby sipped her wine. "Our relationship is important to me," she said carefully. "I just don't know that we need to put a label on it."

He was quiet for a minute, considering her response. "Maybe we don't," he allowed. "But several different people remarked to me today that I had a beautiful family, and it made me realize how much I want you and Emery and Jay to be my family."

She bobbled the glass in her hand, nearly sloshing wine over the rim.

"Now I've freaked you out," he realized.

"Maybe. A little." But she wasn't nearly as freaked out as she should have been, because the truth was, the idea of sharing a family with Julian was far more tempting than she wanted it to be—and *that* freaked her out much more than his declaration. She set the glass down and tucked her feet up under her on the sofa. "It's just that we really haven't been…together…very long."

He held her gaze for a long minute. "Does that mean it's too soon for me to tell you that I love you?"

"*Way* too soon." She realized, as soon as the words were out of her mouth, that her response might have been a tad too vehement. The stricken expression on his face only confirmed it.

"Apparently I don't need to ask if you feel the same way," he remarked dryly.

"Julian…" she said, aching for both of them.

"It's okay." He set his glass of wine aside with hers. "I don't need to be placated."

"I'm not trying to placate you," she denied. "But I'm also not trying to hurt you. You have to know I care about you. A lot."

"Yeah," he said. "I guess I do."

"But you're moving too fast and pushing for something I'm not ready to give," she told him, desperate to explain.

He nodded abruptly. "Point taken."

"I don't know what else to say to you," she admitted. "I wasn't prepared to have this conversation tonight."

"I didn't realize you needed designated prep time before talking to me about our relationship." There was an uncharacteristic edge to his voice, and it sliced through her heart.

"Please understand, Julian. You're the first person—the first man—I've let myself get close to since my divorce. And I'm worried that we might be rushing things a little."

He was silent for a minute, considering, before he asked, "Do you want to take a step back?"

The question surprised her—and maybe even unnerved her a little. Because she was still marveling over the fact that she'd found a man as wonderful as Julian and she definitely didn't want to lose him.

"That isn't what I said," she protested.

"Which isn't an answer to my question," he pointed out.

She shook her head. "No, I don't want to take a step back."

He exhaled audibly, assuring Ruby that wasn't what he wanted, either.

"But…"

There were other factors to consider, other hearts at risk in addition to their own. Most notably, Emery's and Jay's. Both kids were already growing attached to him, and both kids would be hurt if Ruby and Julian's fledgling relationship didn't work out. And the longer she let things go on, the greater the potential damage if it fell apart.

"…maybe we should," she concluded.

# Chapter Eighteen

*Bronco, Montana*

Stanley was on a mission. He knew that if he was going to find his missing bride—and he was—then he needed something more concrete than cryptic messages in a dream. So he drove to Bronco Heights, to the house where Winona's daughter, Dorothea, lived with her daughter, Wanda.

"Stanley." His almost-daughter-in-law greeted him with a hug before ushering him into the warmth of her home.

He removed his boots and coat before following her to the kitchen for the coffee she offered.

"I'm guessing you're here because you talked to Evan," she said as she brought two mugs to the table and took a seat opposite him.

Stanley nodded.

"He told me about the dream a few weeks ago," she confided.

"The first time he had it?" he guessed.

"No, I'd imagine it was at least the second or third time," she mused. "He would have discounted it as meaningless nonsense the first time. Probably even the second."

"Do you believe he has some of Winona's gift?"

She smiled. "He certainly wouldn't consider it a gift, but yes, I do."

"Not as strong as yours, though?"

"Different than mine," she clarified.

He sipped his coffee. "Do you believe your mother pulled a runaway bride?"

She answered without hesitation. "Not for a minute."

"And yet, when you called to tell me about the letter, you told me that her note made it clear that she'd changed her mind."

"Okay, maybe for a minute," she allowed. "When I first read her letter. Because it was the first I'd heard from her in weeks—since our brief conversation the morning of the wedding—and I'd started to fear that she was lost to all of us forever. And suddenly I had proof in my hand—in her own handwriting—that she was alive, and I was so desperately relieved that I let myself believe the words on the page."

"What happened to change your mind?"

"Let me get the letter for you," she said.

He nodded. It was, after all, the reason he'd come—to read Winona's words with his own eyes.

When she returned with the letter, he pulled the single page out of the envelope and unfolded it to skim the brief words.

"It does look like her handwriting," he admitted.

Dorothea nodded. "You can tell by the loops of the *l*'s and the tails on the *y*'s."

"So you believe she *did* write this?"

"I read that letter over and over again, trying to reconcile the words on the page with what I knew about my mother. I traced my fingers over every letter of every word, and that's when I knew she *didn't* write it. Because the pressure on every letter is the same—as if the pen was never lifted from the page."

Stanley tried to follow her reasoning. "You're suggesting that it wasn't written but traced?"

She nodded again.

"Why didn't you come to me with this? Why would you let me wander, lost, worrying about her?"

"If we're not lost, we cannot be found."

"That sounds like something your mother would say."

"But now that you're here," she said. "I've got something else for you, too."

She retrieved a sketchbook from the counter and slid it across the table to him.

Dorothea was an incredibly talented artist who'd made a name for herself illustrating a series of popular children's books. What Winona was most proud of, though, was her daughter's ability to put on the page detailed images of real people she'd never met and places that she'd never been—proof of her gift.

He opened the cover, studied the sketch for a minute. A house with an old truck parked in the driveway.

"Am I supposed to know what this is?"

"I was hoping you might," she admitted. "Because I don't have a clue."

"You've never been to this house?"

She shook her head.

He flipped a few more pages, stopping at a drawing of a horse. "Are you thinking of buying a horse?"

She laughed. "Definitely not anywhere on my radar."

"A truck?"

She shook her head. "I don't know what the pictures mean, but I think they're connected somehow. I think, if you find the house and the horse and the truck, you'll find my mother."

"It might be easier if you'd put a number on the house or a license plate on the truck."

"Nothing worth having comes easy. But I can tell you not to go to Oregon. She's not there."

He didn't ask how she could be so certain, because it was apparent that she was, and that was enough for him.

He closed the sketchbook. "Can I take this?"

"Of course. I only wish I had something more to give you."

"You and Evan have given me hope," he said. "And I can't tell you how much I needed that after all these months."

She walked him to the door, hugged him again. "Promise to save me a dance at your wedding?"

"I promise."

# *Chapter Nineteen*

*Tenacity, Montana*

Julian wasn't proud of the fact that he'd walked out on Ruby after she'd decided to put on the brakes, but he'd been afraid that if he stuck around, the trajectory of their conversation would have gone from bad to worse. And as much as it hurt to hear her say that they should take a step back, he knew it would be infinitely more painful if she suddenly decided a single step wasn't far enough and wanted to end their relationship.

In the twenty hours that had passed since then, he hadn't reached out, because he hadn't known what to say or where they were supposed to go from here. There had been radio silence on her end, too, though he suspected that was more likely because she was busy with Emery and Jay than that she was tying herself up in knots over what had been said and not said the night before.

In any event, the last thing he was in the mood for was Sunday dinner with his family, but he knew that skipping the meal would only lead to questions he wasn't prepared to answer.

As it turned out, his parents and his siblings were all so busy fussing over his great-uncle that they barely gave Julian a second glance when he arrived.

"*Tío* Stanley." He greeted the old man with a hug. "It's good to know that *Má's* enchiladas inspired you to make the trip from Bronco."

"I'll definitely enjoy those," Stanley said. "But I'm here because I need your help finding my bride."

Julian was taken aback by this announcement—and leery of his uncle's request for his assistance. "Wouldn't you be better off hiring a private investigator?"

Stanley shook his head. "It needs to be me. I need to be the one to find her."

"What makes you think I can help?"

"I'm not sure I can explain it in a way that's going to make any sense to you," his uncle admitted.

"Try," Julian suggested.

"She told me to come to you."

He was taken aback. "You've talked to her?"

"Not directly," Stanley admitted. "Look, I get that you're probably already thinking I'm a crazy old man, but I need you to listen with an open mind. Okay?"

"Okay," Julian agreed cautiously.

"You know that Winona has a gift."

"That seems to be the consensus."

"Well, apparently her psychic abilities run in the family. Her great-grandson, Evan, is a skeptic, though, who hasn't embraced his talent. Nevertheless, he came to me a few weeks back because he had a dream…"

Julian listened patiently as his great-uncle recounted what Evan had told him, and then about his visit with Dorothea and the pictures she'd sketched.

Though he wasn't entirely convinced that Stanley was on the right path, he couldn't fault him for wanting to chase down any and every lead. If it was Ruby who'd disappeared, he wouldn't leave any stone unturned in his efforts to find her.

But he knew exactly where Ruby was—and she'd made it clear that she needed some time and distance to figure out her feelings for him. So maybe the best thing Julian could do right now was give it to her.

And even if *Tío* Stanley was on a wild goose chase, Julian figured there wasn't any harm in spending a few days with the man. At the very least, it'd help keep his mind off Ruby.

"I can't believe I let you talk me into this," Julian said, sliding behind the wheel of his truck the next morning.

"I don't think I talked you into anything," Stanley said. "I think you were looking for an excuse to get out of town."

Julian scowled at that, though he couldn't deny that there might be some truth in the old man's statement. Instead he said, "Where are we going?"

"Gray Horse."

"That's rather imprecise."

Stanley shrugged. "I don't have an exact address."

"Do you have anything other than a vague idea based on sketches and dreams?" he asked, punching the name of the town into his navigation app.

Instead of answering his question, Stanley asked one of his own. "Have you ever been in love, Julian?"

Immediately his mind went to Ruby. Because whether or not she was ready to accept his feelings, there was no denying that he was head over heels for the single mom and her kids.

"Yeah," he admitted.

Stanley nodded. "If someone took the woman you loved away from you, what would you do to get her back?"

*Anything*.

Which, he suspected, was his uncle's point.

"So… Gray Horse," he said, turning his truck in the requisite direction.

"Thank you."

"I just want you to be prepared for the possibility that this might not turn out the way you hope."

"I'm going to find Winona," Stanley said confidently. "Not finding her isn't an option."

It was almost lunchtime on Monday before Ruby realized that she'd left her cell phone in her car when she'd gone into work. Of course, her hands had been full, with Jay and all his requisite baby paraphernalia, so it wasn't surprising.

Or maybe she'd forgotten the phone on purpose—a subconscious attempt to prevent herself from checking the screen every five minutes to see if there was a message from Julian. And eliminate the temptation to reach out to him.

But she wasn't happy about the way they'd left things Saturday night and, as a result, she hadn't slept well since then.

He'd told her he loved her and she'd responded by telling him that she wanted to take a step back.

But was she supposed to say the words back to him when she really didn't know how she felt?

How would that be fair to either of them?

The fact was, no matter how many times she went over their conversation in her head, she couldn't make it play out any other way.

But she knew she'd hurt him, and she was sorry for that.

So when Chrissy stopped by the desk for a minute, Ruby left her to keep an eye on the baby while she hurried out to her SUV to retrieve her phone.

When Chrissy moved on, Ruby finally let herself steal a peek at her screen, her heart skipping a beat when she saw that she'd missed a call from Julian.

Actually three calls.

And he'd left one message.

She tapped the screen to access her voicemail.

*Hey, Ruby...*

Just hearing those two words in the warm, familiar timbre of his voice made her knees weak.

Was it any wonder that hearing him say "I love you" had completely unnerved her?

But why had she reacted so strongly to his declaration?

Why was she so reluctant to believe that his feelings could be real?

Or maybe the problem wasn't his feelings but her own.

Because if she let herself believe that he loved her, then she'd have to admit that she was more than halfway toward falling in love with him, too.

And loving Julian would require opening up her heart—a heart that was still a little battered and bruised as a result of being knocked around by her ex-husband during their short-term marriage.

*...Talk soon.*

When the message ended, she realized that her mental meandering had prevented her from actually hearing any of it.

She tapped the replay prompt.

*Hey, Ruby. I was hoping to talk to you before I left, but obviously you're not available right now. Anyway, my great-uncle from Bronco showed up unexpectedly and asked for my help with something, so it looks like I'm going to be heading out of town for a few days. I don't expect I'll be gone any longer than that, but I'll be in touch as soon as I get back. In the meantime, give Emery and Jay big hugs from me. Talk soon.*

She frowned at her phone, as if it was somehow responsible for the frustratingly vague message.

An unnamed relative showed up to ask for help with an unspecified *something* that required him to leave town for *a few days*.

If she didn't know better, she'd think that Julian was trying to put some distance between them.

And maybe she didn't know better.

They'd been together only a few weeks, and while they'd spent a lot of hours together in those weeks, it still wasn't a lot of time in the overall scheme of things.

Maybe there wasn't any mysterious errand and he had plans to hook up with another woman.

She immediately felt guilty for letting such a thought cross her mind, because Julian had proven to her, over and over again, that he was nothing like her ex-husband.

Still, it was possible that he'd changed his mind about what he wanted. That when he'd taken some time to think about their relationship, he'd realized it had gotten too real too fast.

After all, he was a single man who'd just bought his own ranch and she was a divorced mom of a four-year-old and a three-month-old foster child. There were days that, if she didn't love Emery and Jay to bits, she might think about running away, too.

Except that theory didn't jibe with what she knew about Julian, either. Since New Year's Eve, he'd been there for her and her kids. And not just for the fun stuff, either. In the short period of time that they'd been together, he'd seen that her life wasn't all Candy Land and story time snuggles. He'd borne witness to broken appliances and sick kids and stinky diapers. And he hadn't flinched at any of it.

Was it any wonder that she'd fallen in love with him?

She sank into her chair behind the counter, the realization hitting like a sucker punch to her gut.

*She loved Julian.*

Because apparently not wanting to fall in love didn't stop it from happening.

They spent the night at the only roadside motel in the tiny dot on the map known as Gray Horse, sleeping in matching twin beds that were quite possibly as old as the ancient motel.

Julian did not have a good night's sleep.

But maybe it wasn't entirely the fault of the bed.

Maybe it was thoughts of Ruby that had kept him awake.

His mom had always said he led with his heart, as if that was a good thing. But he suspected that leading with his heart in his relationship with Ruby had scared her off.

He glanced at his phone, hoping for another message and experiencing a quick pang of disappointment that there was nothing new. The last communication from her was the text she'd sent the day before.

Enjoy your time with your uncle.

Well, he hadn't expected a string of heart emojis or a row of hugs and kisses, but something a little more personal would have been nice.

Was she annoyed that he'd gone?

But why would she be?

She was the one who said she needed time and space, and he was giving it to her.

"This isn't the right place."

Stanley's abrupt announcement interrupted Julian's musings.

"What is the right place?" he asked.

"I don't know," his uncle admitted.

It had occurred to Julian that *Tío* might not be in control of all his faculties, but notwithstanding his advanced age, he seemed lucid enough. Disregarding the fact that he was relying on dreams and sketches as some sort of mystical compass that he believed would lead him to his AWOL bride, of course.

They decided to stop at the little café beside the motel for breakfast before continuing their journey.

"Where to next?" Julian asked, as his uncle studied a map of Montana.

"Pony Crossing."

"You're just picking random towns with horse names, aren't you?"

"Dorothea's sketch of that horse means something."

"Maybe it means that Winona is somewhere near horses—which narrows our search down to…most of the Western states," Julian noted.

"Well, I know she's not in Oregon," Stanley said.

"And how can you be certain that she's not in the one place that you have actual evidence suggesting otherwise?"

"The postmark's a red heron."

"You mean a red herring?"

His uncle waved a hand dismissively. "Whatever."

Julian swallowed another mouthful of coffee, desperate for the caffeine to kick-start his sluggish brain.

In the light of a new day, he found himself questioning his willingness to accompany Stanley on this search. But *Tío*'s enthusiasm had been infectious, his determination inspiring, and maybe Julian had been feeling a little bit hurt by the realization that while he was preparing to go all in with his relationship with Ruby, she was pulling back.

"You're eager to get home," *Tío* guessed now.

He was, and yet—

"There's nothing I need to rush back for," he said, wishing it wasn't true.

"Not even the special lady in your life?"

"She can manage just fine without me."

"Is that what's bothering you?"

"I'm not bothered."

"You're definitely bothered."

Julian suspected his clenched jaw only supported his uncle's conclusion.

"Sometimes it helps to talk things through," Stanley said.

"If I wanted to talk, I would," Julian assured him.

"Just one more reason I wish Winona was here. You wouldn't have to tell her what was wrong, she'd know."

"Okay, fine. I'm bothered," Julian said. "I wish she needed me, but she doesn't. She's made that perfectly clear."

"But does she want you?" *Tío* asked.

"What?"

"It seems to me that it's more important to be wanted. To be chosen."

Something to think about, Julian mused, before shifting his attention back to his uncle. It was obvious that the old man was hurting, and he feared that Stanley would experience more heartache before this journey was over.

"Maybe we should go home, *Tío*," he suggested gently.

The old man's jaw set. "Not without Winona."

So Julian bit his tongue to hold back any further arguments.

Because he knew as well as anyone that love was sometimes stronger than reason.

# Chapter Twenty

"Is Unca Julian coming tonight?" Emery asked, gliding the soapy sponge over Jay's round belly.

"Not tonight," Ruby said. "He had to go out of town."

"Will he come tomorrow?"

"I don't know. He said he was going to be busy for a few days."

Emery pouted.

"Don't get soap in his eyes," Ruby cautioned, attempting to refocus her daughter's attention on the task at hand while her own mind wandered.

She should have anticipated this.

She should have been careful.

Emery hadn't seen much of her dad since the divorce, and it was a source of continued frustration for Ruby that he rarely chose to exercise his visitation rights.

She helped rinse the soap off the baby, then lifted him out of the infant bath and into a soft hooded towel. Emy helped pat him dry, and it pleased Ruby to see how gentle her daughter was with Jay.

As she guided Emery through diapering and dressing the baby, her thoughts drifted again.

The last time Emery had seen her dad was her birthday in September. Ruby wanted to give Owen credit for remembering the day his daughter was born, but she suspected his mother had reminded him of the date. Caroline had probably bought and wrapped the gift that he brought for the birthday girl, too.

But he'd stayed only long enough to watch her open her present and accept the hug and thanks she gave him, then he was gone.

Sadly, his daughter was unfazed by his departure.

Or maybe she'd just been excited about the cake.

And then Owen hadn't even made an appearance over the Christmas holidays, because he'd been on a beach somewhere with his latest companion. He'd sent a bag of gifts, though. Or maybe it was more accurate to say that a bag of gifts had shown up for Emery with his name on the tags.

In any event, there wasn't much Ruby could do to make her ex-husband want to be a better dad. All she could do was temper Emery's expectations in an effort to lessen her disappointments.

But she hadn't done the same thing regarding Julian. And over the past three-and-a-half weeks, he'd been an almost daily presence in all of their lives.

He'd shared cooking and cleanup duties with Ruby. He'd played games with and read bedtime stories to Emy. He'd prepared bottles for Jay and even changed a few diapers. In short, he'd been a part of their family.

It was hardly surprising that Emery was disappointed to learn that she wasn't going to see him tonight.

And it was Ruby's fault.

She shouldn't have let her daughter get attached to someone else who might disappear from her life—as Julian had apparently done.

And as Jay would eventually do, too.

As much as Ruby hated to admit it, she might have made a mistake when she agreed to take the baby. Not because she didn't love him, but because she *did*—and she knew that Emery did, too. She also knew that their world was going to be left with a very big hole in it if his birth mother was found or another relative came forward or even if Family Services decided to find another—more permanent—placement for him.

Would they consider her application for adoption if she submitted one? Or would she face all the same barriers that she'd had to overcome to be approved as a foster parent?

Ms. Townsend had noted that the baby had bonded with Ruby—surely that had to count for something. Surely a judge would see that he was part of their family and let them stay together.

When her daughter had started preschool, her family consisted of two people—Mommy and Emery. Since returning to school after the holidays, her drawings reflected an expanded family that included baby Jay. And a dog, because Emy was adamant that she wanted a dog. (Though sometimes the dog had a horn in the middle of its head, making Ruby suspect that her daughter really wanted a unicorn.)

And though Ruby sometimes had a hard time saying no to her daughter, there was no way they could take on the responsibility of a dog right now.

Maybe if Julian—

No, she severed the thought before it had a chance to completely form.

She might not have been able to hold herself back from falling in love with him, but that didn't mean she had to depend on him for anything.

And after Emery and Jay were settled for the night (Emy seeking comfort from her thumb again), Ruby crawled under the covers of her own bed and deliberately stretched out in the middle of the mattress, as if that might somehow prove that she didn't need or want the complication of a man in her life.

But she couldn't deny that she missed him.

Julian had told his boss that he needed a few days to deal with a family situation. Possibly a week, at the most. But he really didn't expect that they'd be gone that long, certain Stanley would recognize the futility of his search before then.

But when he woke up on day three in another crappy motel room in another obscure town—this one called Pinto Trail—his uncle was just as determined as ever to forge ahead.

"We're getting closer," Stanley said. "I can feel it."

So they forged ahead to…Mustang Pass.

And Julian resisted the urge to point out that, after three days of driving, they were now within fifteen miles of the starting point of their journey.

Beside the wooden sign that welcomed them to Mustang Pass was a life-size sculpture of the town's namesake standing on its hind legs, its forelegs pawing in the air.

*Tío* straightened up in his seat when they passed the sign, practically vibrating with excitement.

"Is that a restaurant up ahead?" Stanley asked, as Julian turned onto Main Street.

"Looks like," he agreed. "Do you want to stop for lunch?"

It was barely 11:00 a.m., but they'd been on the road for several hours already and Julian wouldn't mind at least stretching his legs.

"I could eat," Stanley said.

He hoped it was true. Over the past few days, he'd noticed that his uncle's appetite was severely diminished. Perhaps unsurprising, considering everything the old man was going through, but still worrisome.

He pulled into a vacant parking spot on the street, in front of the diner with a neon sign identifying it as the Main Street Grill.

"I need to show you something," *Tío* said to Julian, when the server whose name tag identified her as Denise had taken their orders.

Stanley opened the sketchbook he'd dug out of his duffel bag and thumbed through the pages until he found a drawing of a horse. "Look. It's a picture of the horse sculpture that we just passed. Dorothea drew this picture." His uncle stabbed at the page with his finger. "This proves we're in the right place."

Julian didn't think the sketch was proof of anything, though he thought it was possible that Winona's daughter had driven through Mustang Pass at some time in her life and noticed the statue.

It was equally possible that she'd been sketching the Ferrari logo, though he knew better than to point out that possibility to his uncle.

He smiled his thanks at Denise when she delivered his hot roast beef sandwich with fries and extra gravy. Stanley had opted for a double bacon cheeseburger with onion rings.

"And this house," *Tío* said, flipping to another page in the sketchbook, "is in Mustang Pass. I'm sure of it."

Julian sipped his Coke.

"That house could be anywhere," he felt compelled to point out. *Or nowhere*, he thought.

"The house is here," Stanley insisted. "Winona's here."

Denise returned to the table with a pot of coffee to refill his uncle's mug. As she poured, her attention snagged on the sketchbook open on the table.

"Are you friends of Victor's?" she asked.

"Victor?"

She gestured toward the image on the page. "That looks just like his place on Bridle Drive."

"I told you it was here," Stanley crowed triumphantly.

"How well do you know…Victor?" Julian asked the server, trying not to let on that they didn't know the guy at all.

"Not very," she admitted. "But I've only lived in Mustang Pass a few years, and he was something of a hermit when I first moved to town. Rumor has it that his wife walked out on him and broke his heart, but he's been a changed man since they reconciled a few months back.

"They come in together sometimes for a meal. They really are an adorable couple. He's fond of the fish and chips, and she usually gets the daily special, whatever that might be."

"The woman who comes in with him—would you happen to know her name?" Stanley asked.

Denise pursed her lips, trying to remember. "Winifred, maybe. Or something like that. No—Winnie," she decided. "I've definitely heard him call her Winnie."

Stanley sent his nephew a pointed look.

"It could be a coincidence," Julian cautioned, when the server moved on.

*"Tonterías."*

"Maybe it is BS," he acknowledged. "But if this woman who comes in here with Victor is Winona, she's obviously not being held against her will."

"Nothing is obvious and not everything is as it seems," his uncle said stubbornly.

"Have you ever heard her mention someone named Victor?" Julian asked, trying a different tack.

"Never. And there's no way she met some other guy the morning of our wedding and ran off to marry him instead."

"I'm just asking you to consider the possibility that the situation isn't going to lead to the happy ending you're hoping for."

"Beginning," Stanley said.

"Huh?"

"Winona and me agreed that when we got married, it wasn't a happy ending but a happy beginning."

"I don't wanna go to school today," Emery said, when Ruby set her breakfast on the table in front of her.

Ruby held back a sigh as she refilled her coffee. "Why are you doing this? You love school. And it's Wednesday, so you'll have story time and craft circles and Farmer Brown is visiting with Wilbur the Pig today."

The mention of the pig seemed like it might change Emy's mind, but then she shook her head stubbornly. "I wanna stay home today."

"Well, you can't, because I have to go to work."

"I can go to work with you."

"You would be bored to tears," Ruby said.

"Jay goes to work with you," Em pointed out.

"Jay eats and sleeps and poops," she reminded her daughter.

That got a giggle, then Emery's expression grew serious again. "Will you pick me up from school?"

"Mimi will pick you up from school and then I'll pick you up from Mimi's, like I always do."

"You won't go away?"

"Go away?" she echoed, baffled. "Where would I go?"

The little girl poked at her waffle with her fork. "Where did Unca Julian go?"

"Oh, honey." She set her mug on the counter and sat beside her daughter. "Is that what this is about? Are you missing Uncle Julian?"

Emery nodded. "Where did he go?" she asked again.

"I don't know," she admitted.

"Is he coming back?"

"Of course, he's coming back."

She felt confident in that assertion, because Julian's whole family was in Tenacity. Whether or not he came back to her and Emery and Jay was the unknown, and she wasn't going to make false promises to her daughter in that regard.

"But it might be that when he comes back, he doesn't hang around here as much as he did before."

"Why? Doesn't he like me anymore?"

"Honey, I promise that Uncle Julian likes you just as much as he always did. But sometimes, people get busy with their own lives and they don't have as much time to do the things they used to—or hang out with the people they used to hang out with."

"That's what you say about Daddy," Emery pointed out. "That he doesn't come see me cuz he's busy."

*Busted.*

"Because he *is* busy," she said.

He was also a selfish, self-centered jackass, but she kept that to herself. As Julian had noted, Emery would figure it out on her own soon enough.

"He has to work a lot of hours at the insurance company with Papa," Ruby reminded her daughter gently.

"Papa has time for me."

*Busted again.*

Apparently it was going to be one of those days.

* * *

"Bridle Drive," Stanley reminded his nephew, as Julian fastened his belt. "She said the house was on Bridle Drive."

"I heard what she said," he assured his uncle.

"So why aren't you punching it into your map thingy?"

"Because we need to have a plan before we go racing off to confront a stranger."

"The plan is to get Winona back."

*"Tío,"* Julian said, in that patient tone that was starting to drive Stanley crazy. "I think we should contact the local sheriff's department and ask them to check out Victor."

"I don't need to be patted on the head by any more useless deputies. I know Winona's here, in Mustang Pass."

So Julian punched the street name into his navigation app, and when the route directions loaded, he drove.

And in three minutes, he was turning onto Bridle Drive.

"Look!" Stanley pointed—shoving his hand right in front of Julian's face as he did so. "That's the house from the drawing."

Julian ducked his chin to peer around his uncle's arm and pulled his vehicle over to the curb on the opposite side of the road. The house on which his uncle was fixated did bear an uncanny likeness to Dorothea's sketch—right down to the boxwood hedges in the front yard and the ancient pickup truck in the driveway.

Stanley was already unbuckling his belt.

*"Tío, esperar.* Just hold on a second," Julian cautioned.

"I've been holding on for months," his uncle protested. "My fiancée is in that house, and I don't intend to wait another minute to see her."

"We can't just go barging in there without—"

But he was talking to air, because *Tío* Stanley was already halfway across the street.

Cursing under his breath, Julian pushed open his door and hurried after him.

# Chapter Twenty-One

*Mustang Pass, Montana*

Stanley pounded on the door, his fist knocking on the wood in rapid concert with his heart against his ribs.

Dorothea hadn't sketched a picture of Victor, so he had no idea what to expect. When the door opened, he found himself face-to-face with a man of similar age, a couple of inches shorter with a slighter build. His salt-and-pepper hair was short, his bushy white eyebrows drawn together over pale blue eyes.

"Are you Victor?"

Those pale eyes narrowed suspiciously. "Yeah, but unless you've got Thin Mints, whatever you're selling, we're not buying," he said gruffly.

"I'm not selling anything," Stanley told him. "I'm here for Winona."

Something that might have been fear flickered in the other man's eyes before he squared his shoulders and lifted his chin. "Then you're obviously lost."

He attempted to push the door shut, but Stanley had shoved his foot in the opening.

"Winona!"

Victor threw his weight at the door.

It didn't budge.

"Winona!"

"If you don't get off my property right now, I'm going to call the sheriff's office," Victor warned.

"Goodness, Victor—what is all this yelling?"

When Stanley saw the house that matched Dorothea's sketch, he'd desperately wanted to believe that Winona was there. But apparently there had still been a smidgeon of doubt in his mind, because hearing her voice absolutely staggered him.

"Winona." He pushed past the other man to make his way to her, his gaze drinking her in like a parched man would a glass of water, as his nephew, having finally caught up with him, stepped over the threshold.

Stanley reached for Winona's hands and realized his own were shaking.

"Winona," he said again. "My Winona." He lifted her hands to his lips, kissing each one in turn. "I have missed you so much."

She looked at him warily as she withdrew her hands from his grasp, then turned to the man who'd taken up position beside her. "Who is this man, Victor? Do we know him?"

"Wait a minute," Julian said, stepping forward. "Are you saying that you don't recognize *Tío* Stanley?"

"Should I?"

Stanley exchanged a worried look with his nephew.

"I thought amnesia was something that only happened in books and movies," Julian remarked.

"The doctor said it was induced by traumatic brain injury, caused by my fall," Winona said.

"Do you remember the fall?" Stanley asked gently.

She shook her head. "Not the fall or anything that came before." Then her gaze narrowed. "Did he say your name's Stanley?"

"Yes. Stanley Sanchez."

*"I'm sorry, Stanley,"* she said, the words barely more than a whisper from her lips.

He frowned. "Why are you sorry?"

"I...I don't know," she admitted. "I've tried so hard to remember, but the most I've been able to come up with are occasional snippets of conversations and odd dreams. But I do remember thinking, *I'm sorry, Stanley.*"

"Maybe she's sorry that she left you to be with me," Victor said.

Stanley ignored the other man to take Winona's hands again. "Your name is Winona Cobbs and you're my fiancée."

"Fiancée?" she echoed uncertainly.

"We planned to get married in July, but then you went missing."

"I don't understand... Why would I plan to marry you when I'm already married to Victor?"

His blood ran cold. "You *married* this guy? When *in hell* did that happen?"

She turned to Victor again. "How long have we been married?"

"Well." The other man cleared his throat. "The truth is, we're not actually, officially, married."

Stanley was relieved, but Winona looked stunned.

"What do you mean—we're not married?" she demanded. "There's a picture from our wedding on my bedside table."

Stanley's gaze narrowed.

"Photoshop," Julian guessed.

Victor flushed guiltily.

"I don't understand," Winona said. "What's going on here, Victor?"

"What's going on is that these gentlemen are leaving." Victor opened the door again and gestured with a flourish. "And if they don't, I'm going to have them arrested for trespassing."

"Actually, I think calling the sheriff might be a good idea," Julian said, pulling his phone out of his pocket to do just that.

"The sheriff," Winona echoed, obviously flustered.

"Please, go," Victor said. "You're upsetting my wife."

"You mean your fake wife," Stanley said. "Who's actually my real fiancée."

"This is my fault." Winona rubbed her temples. "If only I could remember."

"It's not your fault," Stanley said gently. "And your memories aren't lost forever."

"How can you know?"

"Because your conscious mind might not remember me, but your heart does. And it reached out to your daughter and your great-grandson so that I would come find you."

"I have…a daughter?"

He nodded.

"Beatrix?"

"That was the name you gave her," he confirmed. "Her adoptive parents named her Dorothea. Some people call her Daisy."

"I have a daughter," she said again, not a question this time.

"You have a daughter, a granddaughter, a great-granddaughter, great-grandson and the next generation is well under way."

Her eyes filled with tears. "And I've forgotten every one of them."

"No," Stanley said. "You haven't forgotten. You just need some time to remember."

"I know this isn't quite what you imagined for your reunion," Julian said to his uncle, while they waited for the sheriff's deputies to arrive. "And I'm sorry."

"I feel…gutted," *Tío* admitted. "I was sure she'd rush into my arms, as overjoyed to see me as I was to see her." He shook his head, his expression bleak. "She doesn't even remember me."

"She will. As you said, she just needs time."

"It's been more than five months."

"Five months during which she lived with a stranger in unfamiliar surroundings, listening to lies about her past and her present," Julian pointed out. "You can't really be surprised that none of that triggered her memories."

"No," he agreed. "But how much longer are we supposed to go on like this? How much longer am I supposed to wait?"

"Do you love her?"

"You know I do."

"So maybe the real question is—how long are you willing to wait for the woman you love?"

"Forever," Stanley admitted.

Julian nodded. If this trip to Mustang Pass with his uncle had taught him nothing else, it had at least taught him to savor every minute with the ones you loved.

For him, that included his parents and brothers and sisters, his aunts, uncles and cousins—his whole family. And when he thought of his future, he knew without a shadow of a doubt that he wanted Ruby and Emery and Jay to be part of his family, too.

Now he just needed to convince Ruby that she wanted the same thing—but he suspected that might be a bigger challenge than finding his uncle's missing bride had been.

Deputy Burrows and Deputy Hernandez decided to separate Victor and Winona to get independent statements from each. To the surprise of Deputy Burrows, Victor indicated that he wanted to make his statement in front of the visitors to his home, certain he could make them understand his motives and his actions.

So now Victor and the deputy were seated on one side of the dining room table, with Stanley and Julian across from them.

"For the protection of everyone here, I'm going to record this interview," Deputy Burrows said, setting his phone in the center of the table. "For the record, we are at the home of Victor Thompson at 490 Bridle Drive in Mustang Pass, our attendance at the residence having been requested by Julian Sanchez, also present with his uncle, Stanley Sanchez. The senior Mr. Sanchez claims to be the fiancé of Winona Cobbs, a resident of Bronco, Montana, who was reported missing the day of her July wedding. He further alleges that the woman Mr. Thompson has been passing off as his wife is the same Winona Cobbs.

"Mr. Thompson's supposed wife does not appear to have any identification, but she has consented to a search of the premises to see if any might turn up. At this time, myself and Deputy Hernandez are proceeding on the assumption that the female resident of this address is, in fact, Winona Cobbs, based on her resemblance to photos of the missing woman provided to our office by the Bronco authorities, official confirmation pending fingerprint or DNA match.

"In the meantime, Mr. Thompson has indicated a willingness to make a statement. Though we are at the early stages of the investigation and don't know if any charges might be warranted, he has been advised of his Miranda rights and waived both his right to remain silent and his right to consult with an attorney."

Deputy Burrows then nodded to Victor. "Go ahead, Mr. Thompson."

"Okay, well, first I should probably confirm that my Winnie is Winona Cobbs. I was a loyal reader and big fan of her advice column, 'Wisdom by Winona.' I liked her spunky style and no-nonsense advice. So when my wife and I started having trouble in our marriage, I decided to write to Winona.

"She printed my letter, and I followed her advice. I complimented Marlene's hair and her clothes and her cooking—even when it was awful. But Marlene said six months of compliments didn't make up for thirty-six years of neglect, and she packed her bags and walked out."

"None of which explains how we've ended up here today," Julian noted.

"In the summer, I saw a notice in the paper about Winona's upcoming wedding," Victor explained. "And the closer it got to the date, the madder I got thinking that the woman who destroyed my marriage was planning her own happily ever after."

"A few lines of advice printed in a newspaper isn't to blame for the breakdown of your marriage," Stanley said.

"Anyway, it's not as if I planned to kidnap her. I just wanted to confront her—to let her know that she wasn't so wise after all.

"So the day of the wedding, I was waiting for Winona outside her house. I just wanted to talk to her, so I grabbed her arm, to make her listen. But she wrenched her arm free and lost her balance. As she fell, she hit her head on the porch railing... I didn't think she hit it too hard, but there was a lot of blood." He shuddered at the memory. "So much blood."

The deputy interrupted at that point to remind Victor of his rights, but he ignored the warning.

"She was just lying there," Victor continued. "Crumpled in a heap on the step, and I thought…I thought she was…dead."

"So why didn't you immediately call nine-one-one?" Stanley demanded.

"Because I was afraid I might have been arrested—"

"*Would* have been arrested," Stanley interjected. "Because you assaulted my fiancée."

"I only wanted to talk to her."

"What happened next?" Julian asked.

"Well, I picked her up and put her in my truck. I was sure no one would believe her death was an accident, so I decided to get rid of her body somewhere far away. But I hadn't been driving for very long when she started to moan. Scared me so badly I nearly ran my truck right off the road.

"I was relieved, obviously, to know she wasn't dead. But I was scared, too, because I knew I'd be in trouble for driving away with her."

"It's called kidnapping," Stanley snapped.

"I didn't mean to kidnap her," Victor insisted.

"What happened when you realized Winona wasn't dead?" Julian prompted.

"Well, I asked her how she was feeling, and she said her head hurt. I told her that she had a nasty fall—cuz that's the truth—and she told me that she didn't remember. I asked her what she did remember, and she didn't seem to know how to answer. I asked her simple questions—like her name and date of birth and where she lived—and she couldn't answer any of them. That's when I realized she had amnesia—just like you see in the movies."

"And that's when you decided to take advantage of her loss of memory to create your own history for her."

"I could hardly tell her the truth, not without causing a whole lot of trouble for myself," Victor said sheepishly.

"How about the worry and heartache that you caused her family? And me?" Stanley demanded.

"I didn't want anyone to worry. That's why I wrote the letter to Dorothea."

"So it was you who wrote the letter," Stanley said, with a pointed look at his nephew.

"I had her copy a passage out of a book—told her that the doctor suggested it would be a good exercise for her mind. Then I picked out the words that I needed and traced them onto a new page."

"In that letter, you said that she was fine. But she was knocked unconscious and lost her memory."

"I treated her good," Victor insisted.

"But why would you?" Julian wondered aloud.

His uncle scowled at him. "What kind of question is that?"

He shrugged. "I'm just wondering why a man who apparently blamed Winona for everything that went wrong in his life would want to set up house with her."

"When we first came back to Tenacity, I was still angry with her," Victor admitted. "But I figured that if she believed she was my wife, I could get her to cook and clean and do all the other things a wife is supposed to do."

"And you blame Winona for the fact that your wife left you?" Stanley muttered.

"But she was really weak at first," Victor continued. "So I had to take care of her before she could take care of me. And I realized that I liked taking care of her. That it felt good to be needed."

"He took good care of me," Winona said, as she reentered the room. "Aside from the fact that everything he told me about my life was a lie. He even took me shopping for new clothes, because someone broke in and stole the entire contents of my dressers and my closet." She frowned now. "But I suspect that was a lie, too."

Victor didn't deny it.

"I'm guessing he picked out your clothes, too," Stanley said. "Because neutral colors are not your style."

"They're not?"

"No," he confirmed. "And where is your jewelry?"

"Right here," Deputy Hernandez said, holding up an evidence bag.

"Is there an engagement ring in there?" Stanley asked. "A white gold band with a round amethyst surrounded by diamonds."

Hernandez nodded. "There is. But I can't give it back to you right now. It's evidence."

"Let him have it," Burrows decided. "This fool here just made a full confession—on tape—so I don't think we're going to need it to get a conviction at trial. And if we do, we'll just subpoena them to come back."

"What's going to happen to Victor?" Winona asked, sounding worried.

"We'll take him to the sheriff's office where he'll be held until formal charges are brought."

"Good," Stanley said.

"But fair warning," Burrows continued. "I suspect the local magistrate is going to order a fitness hearing to determine if he's competent to stand trial."

"What happens if he's not competent?" Stanley wanted to know.

"Then he'll be detained in an appropriate psychiatric facility."

"So long as he stays the hell away from Winona."

She looked at Stanley then, a pleat between her brows. "You really do love me, don't you?"

"With my whole heart," he told her.

"Do I love you?"

"I hope so, considering that you'd planned to marry me before you were kidnapped by Victor."

"Was it going to be a big wedding?"

"Big enough."

"Did I have a fancy dress?"

"I can't say for certain, because you refused to let me see it before the wedding, but I imagine it was fancy enough. You said you'd waited more than ninety years to finally be a bride and you were going to do it right."

"I think I've always wanted to get married, but I never thought I'd fall in love again."

"Again?" He jumped on that single word, as if it proved she had some memories of her past.

Winona frowned. "I think I fell in love when I was very young—hardly more than a girl."

"That's right," he said. "You were seventeen."

She closed her eyes for a minute. "Josiah," she finally said. "He was so handsome. So charming."

Stanley felt as if his heart was breaking all over again.

How was it that she could remember the man she'd loved almost eighty years earlier and not remember him?

Then she opened her eyes again and smiled. "But I think you're even more handsome."

"Do you?" he asked, her kind words a balm to his battered heart.

"Here's the ring," Hernandez said, holding it out to Stanley.

"Oh, that's so pretty," Winona said. "And unique."

"Just like you."

Her cheeks flushed. "You are a charmer, aren't you?"

"I know you don't remember me yet, but you let me put this ring on your finger once before and I'm hoping you'll accept it again—if only for safekeeping."

"I guess that would be okay," she agreed, holding out her left hand.

Stanley gently slid the ring onto her third finger.

But as he pushed the band over her knuckle, she made a soft sound, almost of distress, and looked at him with her blue eyes wide and shimmering with tears.

"Did I hurt you?" he asked, immediately concerned.

"No." Winona shook her head. "You didn't hurt me, Stanley." She lifted her hand then to touch his cheek. "I remember."

"You remember...*me*?"

"I remember *everything*," she said softly, her voice thick with emotion. "It's as if the little bits and pieces that were floating around in my mind finally came together to make my memories." She glanced at the ring again. "We got this at an antique sale. You found it inside an old teapot—a hidden treasure, you said."

"That's right," he confirmed, his heart swelling with joy.

"I remember our first date. We met at that little hole-in-the-wall bar in the valley called—" her brow furrowed as she searched for the name "—Doug's."

He gave her an encouraging nod.

"You were there with your nephew—Felix." She laughed softly. "And we stranded him at the bar when we left with the keys."

Her smile faded and her brow furrowed. "Okay, maybe I don't remember everything," she acknowledged. "But it's starting to come back. And most important, I remember how much you love me—and how much I love you."

His throat was tight. His eyes misty.

He gently removed her hand from his cheek and brought it to his lips. *"Mi corazón."*

"*My* heart," she echoed, and smiled.

# *Chapter Twenty-Two*

*Tenacity, Montana*

Ruby was relieved to note that Emery was in a much better mood when she picked her up from Mimi's. And throughout the ride home, her daughter chatted happily about the events of her day—the highlight of which was the appearance of Wilbur the Pig.

"And one of the craft circles was finger painting and I made a picture of my family," Emery said.

"Did you bring it home so I can put it on the fridge?"

"Uh-huh." She unzipped her backpack and pulled out the picture.

Of course, at this early stage in her artistic development, the people in Emery's drawings and paintings weren't much more than round heads with arms and legs sticking out of them. This time, she'd put four people in the picture.

"You and me and Unca Julian and Jay," Emery said, pointing to each one in turn.

"And a puppy?" Ruby guessed.

Em nodded.

When they got home, Ruby dutifully stuck the picture to the refrigerator with a magnet advertising Pete's Pizza.

"How about stir-fry for dinner tonight?"

"Can we have pa'sghetti?" Emery asked hopefully.

She'd already taken the chicken out of the freezer but decided it would keep.

It had been a challenging day from the start, and though Emery seemed to have bounced back, Ruby decided that if her daughter wanted spaghetti, she was going to make spaghetti.

After dinner they played three games of Candy Land, then she let Emery have bubbles in her bath. During story time, she injected extra enthusiasm into the character voices, determined to make her daughter forget that she liked story time with Uncle Julian best.

"Sweet dreams, Emy." She kissed her forehead, inhaling the familiar scent of baby shampoo and little girl. "I love you."

Emery yawned. "I love you, too, Mommy."

And Ruby knew that she had everything she needed right here.

But she still missed Julian.

When Julian finally arrived back at his parents' house in Tenacity, where Stanley suggested he and Winona spend the night before making the longer journey home to Bronco, he discovered that news of the missing bride's rescue had preceded their arrival. Local TV vans, camera crews, reporters and media bloggers lined the path from the driveway all the way to the front door.

Stanley gallantly held them off and ushered his fiancée into a house overflowing with Sanchezes and all of Winona's family, too.

"Looks like somebody's having a party and didn't invite us," Winona remarked.

"Apologies for the oversight," Nicole said, giving *Tío*'s bride-to-be a warm hug. "Until a few hours ago, we didn't know where to send the invitation."

"Well, I'm glad I made it," Winona said. "Because I'm ready to celebrate. Today is the day I got my life back." She looked at the man by her side then and smiled. "My life and my love."

"But how did you all get here so fast?" Stanley wanted to know.

"Julian called his mom to tell her that you'd found Winona, and she promptly called Denise in Bronco, and then the two of them burned up the phone lines spreading the news and, of course, everyone wanted to be here to welcome her home."

Technically, Tenacity wasn't her home—at least not where she lived. But she'd lived in a lot of different places in her ninety-seven years, and one of the things she'd learned was that home was more about the people than the place.

And all these people here were her family.

She was home.

But even in a house filled with love and laughter, she sensed that something—or maybe someone—was missing.

She made her way through the crowd until she found Julian in the kitchen, mixing up another pitcher of sangria.

"I thought you'd disappeared," she said. "I haven't seen you since we got back."

"It's easy to get lost in this crowd," he noted.

"Well, I've found you now, and I'm glad, because I wanted to thank you for helping Stanley find me."

"All I did was drive," Julian said. "*Tío* did the rest. With help from your daughter and great-grandson, as I understand it."

"He couldn't have done it without you," she insisted. "You were an important part of his journey."

He looked wary. "I was glad to help."

"And you called your family…"

"We weren't sure everyone would be able to make it on such short notice, but they did. Because they know how important you are to *Tío*, and that means you're important to all of us."

"I am humbled and overwhelmed by the love in this house," she said. "But not everyone is here."

He frowned as he scanned the crowd. "Who's missing?"

"The one who holds your heart."

"Ah, well." He looked at his great-uncle's fiancée with new respect—and perhaps a little bit of wariness. Because even if the old woman really was a psychic, that didn't mean he wanted her looking too deeply into his mind. Or his heart.

"Or perhaps I should say the *ones* who hold your heart," Winona mused thoughtfully. "She has a child? Children?"

He nodded, because it was true that Ruby and Emery and Jay all held his heart.

But did he hold any of theirs?

Or had the last few days that they'd been apart reminded Ruby that she could manage just fine without him?

Winona touched a hand to his arm. "They've missed you as much as you've missed them."

"I'm not sure that's possible."

"Trust your heart," she urged. "And hers."

He nodded, not certain how else to respond to her unnerving—but hopefully accurate—insights.

"You'll bring them to the wedding?" Winona prompted.

"Just say when."

"Soon," she promised. "Very soon."

Julian watched as she made her way back to her fiancé, who then escorted her to the buffet table and filled a plate with tamales for her.

"It was a good thing you did for *Tío* Stanley," Nicole said, when she found her son in the kitchen.

His smile was wry. "A few days ago, you said it was a wild goose chase."

She shrugged. "But you bagged the goose."

He chuckled. "Don't let Winona hear you call her a goose."

His mom peered past him to the living room, where the reunited lovebirds were seated side by side, their hands entwined.

"He really does love her," she murmured.

"Did you doubt it?"

"No," she said. "But when I believed she'd willingly left him at the altar, I wished it wasn't true."

"*Tío* Stanley said he knew, the first time he met Winona, that she was the woman he'd love for the rest of his life."

"Your dad said the exact same thing about me," she noted. "The Sanchezes are a romantic lot."

"So maybe it won't surprise you to hear that Ruby's the one for me. And that I've known it since the day I met her."

"You mean the day your friend introduced you to his girlfriend?"

"The very same," he confirmed. "I knew it in my heart—and only a few weeks later, my heart ached, because I knew she was going to marry Owen."

"And so you waited."

"I couldn't do anything else," he said simply.

She took his face in her hands and drew it down to press her lips to his forehead. "Go get your girl. Be happy."

"That's my plan."

But there was one more thing that he needed to do first.

"Did you see the news?" Chrissy asked, when she stopped by the reception desk at Tenacity Inn on Thursday morning.

Ruby held up the newspaper that she'd been perusing while sipping her coffee. "I've got it right here."

"That's old news."

"Well, the *Tenacity Tribune* only publishes once a week."

"Which is why people who want to know what's going on get the details online. Or on TV."

"You know I don't watch the news when Emery's around— she doesn't need to know about all the bad stuff that goes on in the world."

"Well, if you'd watched it last night, you might have seen your boyfriend on TV."

"My... Do you mean Julian?"

Her friend's brows lifted. "How many boyfriends do you have?"

She didn't know how to answer that.

Definitely no more than one, but it was possible the number was now zero.

Because even if Julian had been her boyfriend prior to the Winter Carnival weekend, she didn't know that he was still, and she hadn't heard a word from him in three days.

"Tell me why Julian was on TV," she said to her friend.

"Do you remember hearing about that old woman from Bronco—the fortune teller—who went missing the day of her wedding last summer?"

Ruby nodded.

"Julian found her. Well, him and his uncle, who was the missing woman's fiancé."

"You're kidding."

"Nope."

"Where did they find her?"

"Mustang Pass," Chrissy said. "Can you believe she was so close all this time?"

"It doesn't take three days to get to Mustang Pass," she noted.

Her friend looked puzzled.

Ruby waved a hand. "Never mind."

"Anyway, it turns out the bride-to-be had *amnesia*. She completely forgot not only that she was planning to get married but even the identity of her groom."

"Sounds like the plot of a soap opera," Ruby mused.

"Complete with a hunky hero," Chrissy said with a wink, before she hurried off to check that the conference room was set up for lunch.

Although her friend had already given her the broad strokes of the story, when Chrissy was gone, Ruby opened a browser on the desktop computer to fill in the details.

So much for Julian's promise to be in touch as soon as he got back to town, Ruby mused, as she skimmed the online write-up. And she knew that he was back in town, because there were numerous photos and sound bites to prove it.

Obviously he'd been telling the truth when he said that he had something to do out of town, but not when he'd promised to be in touch as soon as he got back.

But that was okay, Ruby decided. Because she'd been the one to suggest that they take a step back. And if that step back and a few days apart had made him realize his feelings for her weren't as strong as he'd believed, well, that was something better discovered sooner rather than later.

It was even better that she hadn't told him that she loved him, too.

And maybe her heart ached to think that their relationship could be over already, but she would survive.

She'd gotten through the breakdown of her marriage; she had to believe she could get through this.

# Chapter Twenty-Three

"What's for supper?" Emery asked.

"We literally just walked in the door," Ruby noted. "Are you really thinking about supper already?"

"I just wanna know what we're having."

"Chicken fingers."

Her daughter's expression brightened. "The kind like Julian makes?"

"No," Ruby said, as she buckled Jay into his high chair. "The kind that comes in the box from the grocery store."

"Oh." Em's disappointment was palpable.

"But I've got sweet potato fries to go with the chicken fingers. And ice cream for dessert."

"Pink ice cream?"

"Of course."

"With sprinkles?"

*Why not?* Ruby thought.

"Pink ice cream with lots and lots of sprinkles," she promised, putting some soft blocks on Jay's tray to keep him occupied while she prepared dinner. "And don't forget to take your lunchbox out of your backpack before you put it in the closet."

"Then can I watch TV?"

She glanced at her watch. "You can watch one episode of *Paw Patrol*."

"Yay!" Em clapped her hands together.

As she headed into the living room, a knock sounded at the front door.

"Someone's here," Emery announced.

"Let me get it," Ruby said, reminding her daughter of her cardinal safety rule.

"It's Unca Julian!" She bounced on the sofa cushion she was standing on to look out the front window. "He's back!"

Ruby took a deep breath to calm the butterflies suddenly winging around in her belly and smoothed a hand down the front of the dress she hadn't yet had a chance to change out of.

"Open the door, Mommy," Emery urged.

She opened the door, a carefully neutral expression on her face. "Hello, Julian."

He smiled, and her knees quivered. "Hello, Ruby."

He looked tired. She could see it in his eyes and the lines around his mouth, making her think the successful outcome of his trip hadn't been as effortless as the media reports implied.

"I saw you on TV at Mimi's!" Emery announced excitedly.

Which was news to Ruby. Her former mother-in-law was usually as careful as she when it came to protecting Emery from stuff like that, but obviously Caroline had figured the little girl would be interested, because it was about Julian.

"Did you?" he said.

"Apparently you're a local hero," Ruby remarked.

"My ten minutes of fame."

"I thought it was fifteen minutes of fame."

"That was pre–social media," he told her. "When people had attention spans longer than two hundred and eighty characters."

"Fair point," she acknowledged.

He waited a beat before asking, "Are you going to let me come in?"

She finally moved away from the door, carefully sidestepping her daughter, who was jumping up and down, practically dragging him over the threshold.

"I haven't seen you in days and days," Emery said to him. "Where'd you go, Unca Julian?"

"I had to go out of town with my uncle."

The little girl abruptly remembered that she'd been mad, because she fisted her hands on her hips. "You went away and didn't say goodbye."

"It was a last-minute trip," he explained. "And I knew I wasn't going to be gone for very long."

"It was *days* and *days*," she said again.

"It was longer than I expected," he acknowledged. "And I'm sorry for that."

"Mommy says I have to forgive someone when they say they're sorry, so I forgive you. But I'm still mad that you didn't say good-bye."

Julian set down the long cardboard tube in his hand to lift her up so they could continue the conversation eye-to-eye. "Would you stop being mad if I promise to never again leave without saying goodbye?"

"Maybe. If you pinky swear."

"Pinky swear," he said, linking his smallest digit with hers. "I also promise that, any time I go away, I will come back."

She seemed satisfied with this, because she nodded. "Okay."

Then she gave him a smacking kiss on the cheek and wriggled to be let down.

"Are you gonna stay for supper?" she asked, when her feet were on the ground again. "We're having chicken fingers and sweet potatoes and pink ice cream. With sprinkles."

"I'd like to stay," he said, with a questioning glance in Ruby's direction, "but I need to talk to your mom first, to make sure it's okay with her."

"It's okay, isn't it, Mommy?" Emery asked on his behalf.

Ruby narrowed her eyes on Julian as she spoke to her daughter. "Didn't you want to watch *Paw Patrol*, Em?"

"Oh, yeah," she suddenly remembered, skipping into the living room.

Julian held Ruby's gaze. "I'm getting the impression that you're not going to forgive me as easily as your daughter did."

"There's nothing to forgive," she said. "You don't need my permission to go out of town—or anywhere else."

"So why does it seem like you're mad?"

"Because I don't appreciate you making promises to my daughter that you can't keep," she told him. "She's a little girl and she's counting on you to stick around—and maybe that's my fault. Maybe I should have limited the time she spent with you so that she didn't get too close, and I didn't, and that's on me.

"But you have no idea how hard the last few days have been. Every day, she asked about you, and every day, I struggled to answer her questions without giving her false hope."

"The last few days were hard on me, too," he said, taking a step toward her. "I missed you and Em and Jay like crazy."

She took a step back, preserving the distance between them. Because she knew that if she let him get too close, if she let him touch her, she'd forget that she was mad. In fact, she'd likely forget everything but how much she missed being held in his arms.

"But you're the one who left," she pointed out. "And your message said that you'd be in touch as soon as you got back."

"That's why I'm here."

"You got back yesterday."

His brows lifted. "Is that why you're giving me a hard time? Because I waited—" he glanced at his watch "—twenty-two hours before knocking on your door?"

She scowled. "It sounds ridiculous when you put it like that."

And maybe it *was* ridiculous, but she'd been hurt by his disappearing act, and she didn't know what to say or do—or even how to feel—now that he was standing in front of her, as if nothing had changed between them.

"I'm sorry I didn't come sooner, but there was something I needed to do before I could see you."

"You didn't even call."

"Because I missed you like crazy the whole time I was gone," he said again. "And I knew that if I heard your voice, there'd be no way that I could stay away."

The sincerity in his voice, in his gaze, chipped away at her lingering annoyance and knocked down the walls she'd tried to put up around her heart.

"No one said that you had to stay away."

And apparently he heard the softening in her tone, because his lips curved in a hopeful smile. "Did you miss me?"

*More than I ever could have imagined.*

Not that she had any intention of admitting it to Julian.

"You said there was something you needed to do before you could see me," she said instead.

"There was," he confirmed, reaching down to retrieve the cardboard tube he'd set aside earlier.

Her curiosity was immediately piqued. "What's that?"

"If you'll let me past the foyer, I'd be happy to show you."

He removed his boots and coat before making his way into the kitchen. When Jay spotted Julian, he dropped the block he'd been chewing on and gave him a gummy smile.

"Hey there, big guy," Julian said, returning the block to the baby, who immediately dropped it again.

He chuckled. "We'll play that game later," he promised, before popping the cap off the end of the tube he carried to withdraw the papers that were inside.

Blueprints, Ruby realized.

"Remember when I told you that I bought land to start my own ranch?" Julian asked her now.

"Of course." It was the night they'd had to cancel their date because Emery had strep throat. More important, it was the first time in all the years that her daughter had been alive that Ruby hadn't been alone in worrying about her little girl.

"Well, this is the plan for the house I was originally going to build," he told her, unrolling the papers. "Kyle Mitchell, an architect friend of mine, drew them up when he was in college several years back. The assignment was to interview a prospective client and draft a plan in accordance with the client's wishes. I was the prospective client, and he gave me the plans as a tangible reminder of my goals."

She looked at the simple ranch-style house with a wraparound front porch, main floor master bedroom and en suite bath plus an office and an open concept kitchen-living room combination.

"It's nice," she said, though she had no idea why he was showing her old plans for a house.

"But small," he acknowledged.

"Well, how much space do you really need?" she asked reasonably.

"Kyle tried to push me to add at least a second bedroom, but I was worried that if I had a spare room, one of my annoying siblings might want to stay with me."

Ruby couldn't help but smile at that.

"Anyway, Kyle has his own architectural firm in Bronco now, and though he specializes in commercial buildings, he agreed to tweak my old plans for me."

He slid the top page aside so that she could see the revised plan, with two additional bedrooms, a second bath, a bigger kitchen, separate dining room and expanded living space.

"That looks like more than a tweak," she noted.

"Well, once we got talking, I realized that I was going to need a lot more space to accommodate you and Emery and Jay."

Her breath caught in her throat, and she had to swallow before she could respond. "You want us to live with you?"

"Well, not today—or even tomorrow—because it's going to take a little while to build," he confided. "But at the risk of again being accused of moving too fast, yes, I want you and your kids to live at The Start of a New Day Ranch with me."

Joy—pure and unadulterated—filled her heart to overflowing.

"I also want you to marry me—that's just a heads-up, not a

proposal," he hastened to assure her. "I'll save the whole down-on-one-knee thing until you can hear me tell you that I love you without freaking out."

"I didn't freak out," she protested, though without much conviction.

"You totally freaked out," he said, but the smile that accompanied his words assured her that she was forgiven. "But I should have anticipated that my declaration might come as a surprise to you, and I shouldn't have let myself be hurt by your apparent rejection of my feelings."

"I didn't reject your feelings," she denied. "I didn't know what to do with them. And before I had a chance to figure it out, you were gone."

"My uncle needed my help. And I thought you needed some time to figure out how you felt."

"I felt angry that you walked out on me," she told him, unwilling to let him off the hook completely.

He reached for her hands and drew her closer. "I left town," he said gently. "I didn't leave *you*."

"It felt like you'd left me—and Emery and Jay."

"I tried to call you," he reminded her. "And I know you got my message, because you replied by text."

"You're referring to the message in which you said that an unnamed uncle needed your help with an unspecified something which required you to be gone for an indeterminate amount of time?"

"Yeah," he admitted, drawing her closer still. "And now I understand how that might have seemed…inadequate."

She nodded.

"But what you need to understand, *corazón*, is that when I said I loved you, my feelings weren't contingent upon you saying the words back—or on anything else at all." He released her hands now to slide his arms around her. "I said I loved you because it's how I feel. And I will love you forever."

She linked her hands behind his neck. *"También te amo."*

He grinned. "Someone's been brushing up on her Spanish."

"I had some time on my hands while you were away," she said. "And some time to think about how I felt—and why I reacted so strongly when you told me you loved me."

"You mean why you freaked out?" he teased.

"I accused you of moving too fast and pushing for more than I was ready to give, but the truth is, I was scared. Not of your feelings so much as my own. Because I'd only just realized that I'd fallen hard and fast, and I wasn't close to being ready to admit those feelings out loud.

"And then you were gone, and I realized there was something even scarier than the way I felt—the possibility that I might have lost the best man I've ever known."

"Never," he promised, and finally lowered his mouth to hers.

It was a kiss of apology and forgiveness; a kiss of passion and promise; but mostly, it was a kiss of love.

"I really do love you," she told him.

"You want to prove it by being my date for Stanley and Winona's wedding on Saturday?" he asked.

*"This* Saturday?"

He nodded.

"I guess she wasn't kidding when she said she didn't want to wait," Ruby mused.

"So what do you say about being my *plus-three*?" Julian prompted.

Her brows lifted. *"Plus-three?"*

"I know you and Emery and Jay are a package deal, and I wouldn't have it any other way."

"In that case, you've got yourself a *plus-three* for the wedding."

Winona's original wedding dress had been destroyed by Victor, and she was glad, because she wouldn't have wanted to wear it again. Instead, she went to Cimarron Rose, a boho clothing boutique in Bronco, where proprietor Everlee Roberts Abernathy came through for her in a big way. And when Winona walked down the aisle in a stunning gown of crimson lace carrying a bouquet of lavender roses, purple carnations and red gerbera daisies, it was the consensus of the guests that she was a stunning and unique bride. (And that was before she lifted the hem of her skirt to show off the purple cowboy boots on her feet.)

Ruby didn't know that she'd ever seen a more radiant bride— or a groom more obviously in love. And when the elderly couple exchanged their heartfelt vows, she didn't think there was a dry eye left in the church.

"It was a beautiful ceremony," Ruby said to Winona, as she and Julian made their way through the reception line at The Library, the restaurant owned by one of the Bronco Sanchezes. All Winona's family was on the receiving line, including her great-grandchildren Evan and Vanessa.

"Short and sweet." The bride winked at her. "When you've waited more than nine decades to be a bride, you don't want to waste too much time on the vows or you might not live long enough to enjoy your honeymoon."

Ruby had to laugh, even as she felt her cheeks grow warm.

"But don't worry, honey," Winona continued. "Your turn will come before too long." Then the old woman laid a hand on her arm. "He wasn't the first, but he will be the last. And then your family will be complete."

Ruby had heard rumors about the old woman's psychic abilities, of course, but she wasn't entirely sure she'd believed them. Not even after Julian told her about Dorothea's sketches and Evan's dreams. Not until the warmth of Winona's touch seemed to penetrate all the way to her wary heart.

The bringing together of families and friends made a wedding ripe with opportunities for awkward encounters and embarrassing moments. Having already survived one, in her first introduction to the bride and the groom, Ruby tried to brace herself for the next: meeting up with Julian's parents.

Thankfully, that turned out to be neither awkward nor embarrassing. In fact, his parents were warm and welcoming in their greetings, and in no time at all, Nicole was cooing over the baby she'd stolen from her eldest son's arms while Will was being charmed by Emery, leaving Ruby and Julian to simply enjoy the moment and being together.

Bethany McCreery, the wedding singer Stanley and Winona had booked for their July wedding date, was unavailable for their rescheduled nuptials, but she'd previously made a recording of "their song" that she allowed them to play for their first dance. As they swayed together to the music, Winona's eyes sparkled with happiness and Stanley's smile stretched from ear to ear.

After the dancing there was cake. And after the cake had been served, Stanley and Winona mingled with their guests some more, preparing to make their exit from the reception to head off on their honeymoon.

"I need to ask another favor," Stanley said to Julian, when the newlyweds came to say goodbye.

"I don't think so," he said. "I'm still recuperating from the last favor I did for you."

"This one won't require sleeping in uncomfortable motel rooms," *Tío* promised.

"What is it?" he asked warily.

"Check out the real estate listings in Tenacity while we're on our honeymoon." The old man slid an arm across his new wife's shoulders. "Me and Winona have decided to split our time between Bronco and Tenacity when we get back from our honeymoon."

"Why would you do that? Don't you want to slow down and take some time to just enjoy being together?"

"Slow is for old people," Winona said with a wink.

"And we definitely plan to enjoy being together," Stanley said.

"But there are people in Tenacity who could use my guidance," the bride said.

"And maybe my help, too," her groom added.

"What is it you plan to do, *Tío*?" Nicole asked.

"I'm going to help find missing persons. After all, I found Winona when no one else could."

Julian considered reminding him that he'd found his bride because her daughter and grandson had given him all the clues, but he figured the old man's plans were harmless and that everyone should have a hobby.

"Are you really interested in detective work?" Nina asked her great-uncle.

"I really am," Stanley said. "And I've always had a knack for solving puzzles."

"In that case, I might have your first case for you."

"Tell me about it," he urged.

She shook her head. "It can wait until you get back from your honeymoon."

"Can't you at least give me a clue?"

"Alright," she relented. "It involves history and a mystery... and a long-lost love."

Stanley rubbed his hands together. "Sounds like just the kind of juicy case a hungry investigator could sink his teeth into."

"*After* his honeymoon," Winona said firmly.

"*Si, querida,*" he dutifully intoned, making everyone laugh.

"And here comes your ride," Luca chimed in, as an antique car with a "Just Married" sign on the back and streamers of cans hanging off the rear bumper pulled up in front of the restaurant.

"Thank you all for being here to celebrate with us today," Winona said, waving to the crowd of guests.

"Haven't you forgotten something?" Marisa asked, with a pointed glance at the bouquet in the bride's hand.

"I guess I have," Winona said with a laugh. "Come on, all you single women. Gather around for the ceremonial bouquet toss."

"You're not going to vie for the prize?" Julian asked Ruby, when she held herself back from the group of women pressing forward. A group that included Winona's almost eighty-year-old daughter, Dorothea.

"If my mother can find love again at her age, perhaps there's hope for me to do the same," she said, as she playfully elbowed her way to the front of the crowd.

But Ruby only shook her head as she put one arm around her daughter and tucked the other into the crook of Julian's arm, where the baby was sleeping. "I've already got everything I want right here."

Winona turned her back to the group and tossed the flowers over her shoulder.

The bride proved to have an impressive arm, because the bouquet sailed over the heads—and outstretched hands—of the group of single women to smack Ruby in the chest.

"You caught the flowers, Mommy," Emery exclaimed.

Apparently she had, though it had been a reflex more than anything that caused her fingers to clutch the flowers before they could fall to the ground.

"I guess that means you're next," Nina Sanchez said.

"Next after me, maybe," her sister, Marisa, chimed in, reminding everyone that she and Dawson would be exchanging their vows the very next Friday, having snagged the Tenacity Social Club for their after-party when another event was canceled.

"I'm not in any hurry," Ruby assured them. But she tipped her head back against Julian's shoulder then and smiled at him. "But I'm no longer opposed to the idea of another walk down the aisle, either."

"Meeting the right man makes all the difference," Daphne Cruise said, with a loving glance at her husband, Evan.

"It really does," his sister, Vanessa, agreed.

"Lucky for me," Ruby said, pitching her voice for Julian's ears only. "I met the best man of all."

# *Epilogue*

*Valentine's Day*

He opted for red flowers this time, because they seemed more appropriate for the occasion. Red roses, white lilies, miniature red carnations and white chrysanthemums. He wanted to do something special for their first Valentine's Day together, but though there was a ring burning a hole in his pocket, Julian hadn't yet decided whether he would pull it out tonight. As eager as he was to move forward with plans for their future, he was conscious of Ruby's desire to take things slow.

As he approached her house, another vehicle was pulling out of her driveway. The driver smiled and waved as she passed going in the opposite direction.

Julian picked up the bouquet of flowers and made his way to the front door, sliding the key Ruby had given him only a few days earlier into the lock. She'd acted like the key was no big deal, but he knew it was, because it was tangible proof that she wasn't going to shut him out again.

"Mommy, Unca Julian's home!"

He managed to save the flowers as Emery leaped into his arms. He was sure he wouldn't always get such an exuberant welcome from the little girl, but he knew he'd never grow tired of it.

"Was that Ms. Townsend from Family Services I saw leaving just now?" he asked, as Ruby made her way into the foyer.

"It was," she confirmed.

Julian was having a little trouble deciphering her nonverbal clues, because her lips were curved but her eyes were shiny with unshed tears. He cautiously offered her the flowers. "Happy Valentine's Day?"

She laughed as she accepted the bouquet. "Thank you." She rose on her toes to brush her lips against his. "These are undeniably the second-best gift I got today."

"What else did you get?"

"Very good news. Family Services has approved my application to adopt Jay."

"That means he gets to stay with us forever," Emery chimed in.

"Definitely the best Valentine's Day gift," Julian agreed.

She nodded. "There's nothing I want more than for Jay to be my son—officially and legally—except maybe to make him *our* son."

His heart gave a cautious leap of joy inside his chest. "And how would we go about that?"

"The easiest way would be to get married," she said, her tone deliberately casual.

"You think marriage would be easy?" he asked, only half-teasing.

"Well, loving you is the easiest thing I've ever done, so I figure being married to you should be a piece of cake."

He grinned. "A piece of wedding cake?"

"Can we have choc'ate cake?" Emy piped up to ask.

Ruby had to laugh. "We can have whatever kind of cake you want, if Julian says *yes*."

"Say *yes*," the little girl urged.

"Why don't you take these flowers into the kitchen for your mom?" Julian said, handing her the paper-wrapped bouquet.

"Okay."

The happy light in Ruby's eyes dimmed a little as her daughter disappeared from sight.

"You're not going to say *yes*," she realized. "You wouldn't have wanted Emery out of the room if you were going to say *yes*."

He took her hands and drew her toward him. "I don't think I could ever say *no* to you. But I also couldn't let you hijack the proposal I'd been planning."

"There's no way you were planning to propose."

"No way, huh?" He pulled the ring out of his pocket and dropped to one knee.

Ruby's eyes grew wide at the sight of the sparkling diamond set in a simple gold band. The stone was on the smallish side, not intended to make a statement about anything other than the sincere love in his heart.

*"Ohmygod."* She pressed a hand to her heart.

"I hope you know by now that I love you, Ruby."

She nodded, her eyes glittering with emotion. "And I love you."

"So what do you say—will you marry me?"

"Yes." She responded to his question without hesitation. "Yes, Julian, I will marry you."

Emery came back as he was sliding the ring on Ruby's finger. "What happened, Unca Julian? Did you fall down?"

Her mom choked on a laugh.

"Actually, I did," he said. "I fell head over heels for your mom and you and your brother."

The little girl's brow furrowed. "Did you hurt your head? Do you want me to kiss it better?"

"I think a kiss right here—" he tapped a finger to his cheek "—would make me feel much better."

She dutifully kissed his cheek, and gave him a hug, too, for good measure.

Julian rose to his feet then. "Now that we're officially engaged," he said, snaking an arm around Ruby's waist to pull her close. "How about setting a date for our wedding?"

"What's your hurry?" she wondered.

"Only that I don't want to spend a single day of the rest of my life without you."

"Married or not, you're stuck with me now, cowboy." She lifted her arms to loop them over his shoulders and draw his mouth to hers. *"Soy tuyo para siempre."*

\* \* \* \* \*

*Look for*
The Maverick's Promise
*by Melissa Senate,*
*the first installment in the new continuity*
*Montana Mavericks: The Tenacity Social Club*
*on sale February 2025, wherever Harlequin*
*books and ebooks are sold.*

*And catch up with the previous books in*
*Montana Mavericks: The Trail to Tenacity*

Redeeming the Maverick
*by* New York Times *bestselling author Christine Rimmer*

The Maverick Makes the Grade
*by* USA TODAY *bestselling author Stella Bagwell*

That Maverick of Mine
*by Kathy Douglass*

The Maverick's Christmas Kiss
*by JoAnna Sims*

The Maverick's Christmas Countdown
*by Heatherly Bell*

*Available now!*